D1626044

RICHARD HAPPER

REASONS TO LOOK ON THE
BRIGHT SIDE

PORTICO

To my son Harry, for helping me look on the bright side of even the cloudiest day.

First published in the United Kingdom in 2012 by
Portico Books
10 Southcombe Street
London
W14 0RA

An imprint of Anova Books Company Ltd

Illustrations by Sam Bevington

ISBN 9781907554681

A CIP catalogue record for this book is available from the British Library.

10 9 8 7 6 5 4 3 2 1

Printed and bound by 1010 Printing International Ltd, China

This book can be ordered direct from the publisher at
www.anovabooks.com

'If life gives you lemons, make lemonade.'

Dale Carnegie

INTRODUCTION

They say you can't make a silk purse out of a sow's ear, and maybe they're right. But you can take the rest of the pig and make a pretty awesome bacon sandwich.

Happy accidents happen all the time and sometimes the sun really does come out tomorrow. You don't believe me?

Well, consider the Korean Demilitarized Zone, a terrifying stretch of no man's land stuffed with landmines, razor wire and watched by some seriously paranoid soldiers. It's so scary that no one goes in – which, in a weirdly wonderful way, makes it an Eden-like refuge for the extremely rare Korean Tiger, the beautiful Amur leopard and 320 species of birds that would no doubt he hunted to the point of extinction anywhere else.

Even life-and-death situations can have their bright side. It was only when President James Garfield was shot and doctors couldn't find the bullet that Alexander Graham Bell had the idea of inventing the metal detector.

With a bit of dedication, it's even possible to create your own

good luck. A tax on cocoa beans in Italy made chocolate so expensive that patisserie owner Pietro Ferrero was forced to experiment with the one ingredient he had lots of – hazelnuts – and he ended up inventing Nutella ... sweet.

Whatever you do, don't give up. Some catastrophes take a while to turn good but they get there in the end. For example, Britain was furious when Germany scuttled all her battleships in Scapa Flow at the end of World War I. But we're delighted that the wrecks are now one of the world's premier dive sites, home to much amazing marine and exotic wildlife.

So don't worry if life deals you a bum hand; maybe you're meant to put your foot in it. The thing is to be prepared. Then when disaster strikes you will know how to spot the bright side. To help you, I here present a year's worth of the greatest, the funniest and the most wonderfully shiniest of all silver linings from history's darkest clouds. Enjoy this book ... and remember to always look on the bright side of life!

JANUARY

DICK FINALLY GETS SATISFACTION

1 Today in 1961, Decca Records auditioned a small Liverpool band in their London studios. Eventually, however, they decided the group wasn't sellable. 'Guitar groups are on their way out,' Decca representative Dick Rowe told the band at the time. Not long after, the group signed with EMI. Its name? The Beatles. However, Mr Rowe later made good on his gaffe by asking the guitarist of the group, George Harrison, if he knew any other bands worth signing. George kindly pointed him in the direction of a certain pouty individual called Mr Michael Jagger ...

IF ... YOU CAN KEEP YOUR HEAD

Leander Jameson was Administrator General of Matabeleland when he was given a very special mission. Cecil Rhodes, Prime Minister of Cape Colony, wanted him to stir up trouble to help overthrow the neighbouring Transvaal government. The 'Jameson Raid' was a total failure, sparking the Boer War. Jameson himself was captured today in 1896. But some qualities in this quixotic character caught the eye of one Rudyard Kipling, and inspired him to write what is possibly the most popular poem in English – *If*.

COMPUTER SAYS NO ...

It was the early 1970s and a couple of computer geeks, both called Steve, were mucking about with prototype video games. Using some spare parts, they also built a little computer in their garage, which they showed to games manufacturer Atari. The company rejected it outright, so the twenty-somethings decided to market and sell it themselves. Which worked out rather nicely. They incorporated their company today in 1977 and, by 2011, Apple was worth around $300 billion.

SITTING PRETTY

At the 1987 New York Chair Fair, the judges deliberated for hours before awarding one of the top prizes to Tom Musorafita. To their embarrassment, it turned out that he wasn't a promising designer, but a construction worker. He had seen the entries being delivered and, for a laugh, decided to knock one up himself out of bits from his skip. For fans of unpretentious art, Tom's hotchpotch of a cardboard drum, a green bin lid and some plasterboard was a triumph.

CHEERS, CHARLIE

Today in 1477, the Duke of Burgundy came to a sticky end at the Battle of Nancy. Not much of an upside there, you might think. But as a result Burgundy became part of France. Later, its ecclesiastical vineyards were sold off to the bourgeoisie. The Napoleonic inheritance laws resulted in further subdivision of the best holdings. Eventually this created a profusion of small family-owned wineries. And it's this small-but-beautiful way of growing grapes that makes the wine of Burgundy so famous – and delicious – today.

IN THE HOT SEAT

6 Menelik II of Ethiopia was a famously forward-looking emperor. He championed the country's independence and, when he heard about the invention of the electric chair in America (patent filed today in 1897), he supposedly ordered three to dispatch ne'er-do-wells in his kingdom. However, he overlooked the fact that Ethiopia had no electrical power industry to make the chairs work. Rather than waste his investment, Menelik simply used one of the chairs as a thoroughly modern throne.

NOT MY BEST WORK

7 Bad news for the creators of the film *21 Days*, which was released today in 1940. The *Spectator's* film critic was none other than literary legend Graham Greene and he gave the film a scathing review. He called its writing banal and said the film was 'slow, wordy and unbearably sentimental'. However, anyone fearing for the poor screenwriter's mental health was promptly cheered up by the fact that Greene admitted at the end of the review that he himself had written the screenplay.

ZERO TOLERANCE

Andrew Jackson began his career as a land speculator in Tennessee. When he was swindled on a large deal he was left owing thousands. From that day on he loathed debt. So, when he became US President, Jackson set about eliminating the $58 million national debt. For six years he sold government assets and cut costs like a fiend, and today in 1835 he announced that, for the *first and only time in history*, the US national debt was $0. In 2012, it is $14.2 trillion.

IN THE PINK

Horatio Bottomley was a businessman, MP, journalist and crook. He founded a host of companies designed chiefly to separate investors from their money, and he was constantly going bankrupt or being sued. Staring one particularly sticky scandal in the face, Bottomley decided to generate some positive publicity for his projects. So, today in 1888, he founded a paper aimed at City financiers, full of puffery for his own schemes. And so was born that peerless journal of respectability, the *Financial Times*.

THE TUBE TAKES OFF

10 The 19th-century railway boom made long-distance travel much easier, but a Parliamentary Commission banned railways from operating in much of Inner London – to protect the precious architecture – so the capital's termini were on the outskirts of the city. This was a hassle for travellers, and increased road traffic congestion in the capital. Something had to be done, but how to get round that Commission order? And so, today in 1863, the Metropolitan Railway opened – the world's first underground railway.

DON'T DO IT, MIKE

11 Today in 1984, Radio 1 DJ Mike Read was playing the nation's No. 6 record when he suddenly decided it was obscene and stopped the track. Perhaps he hoped banning the song would deter listener interest. But, far from damaging sales, the hitherto modestly successful song, 'Relax' by Frankie Goes to Hollywood, shot to No. 1 for five weeks and became the 7th best-selling UK single of all time. The group's next two singles went straight to No. 1. Suck to that, DJ.

MONEY (THAT'S WHAT I WANT)

12 Berry Gordy was a struggling 1950s songwriter when he suddenly scored a big hit when he wrote 'Lonely Teardrops' for Jackie Wilson. But he earned hardly any money from the record company – basically, he'd been stiffed. So, borrowing $800 from his family, he set up his own label, creating Tamla Records today in 1959 and Motown Records a year later. In the next decade, Motown and Tamla would have hundreds of Top 10 hits all over the world.

LE PLUS GRAND RADIO

13 Ah, the fickle French – just 20 years after the Eiffel Tower was built in 1889, it was going to be torn down. Visitors loved it, but many Parisians loathed its mighty iron frame, dwarfing the city's other monuments, and it seemed the government would indeed pull the landmark down. However, the same height that caused such problems also brought its salvation – today in 1908, the tower proved matchless as a home for the recently invented radio transmitter and the world's most phallic tourist attraction was reprieved.

DOWN BUT NOT OUT

14 When Australian cricketer Bill Woodfull was hit under his heart in an Ashes Test today in 1933, it nearly sparked a riot. England were countering the brilliant batting of Don Bradman and other Aussies by bowling fast and short – Bodyline. The tactic was hated by Australians, but Woodfull's injury and the dignified way in which he responded to the 'unsportsmanlike' bowling turned even English opinion against bodyline. After England's return, the sport introduced new laws preventing bowlers targeting batsmen. Cricket was a gentleman's game once more.

SLOANE'S TREAT

 Imagine the outrage today if a wealthy baronet died and his estate was given £1.7 million by the taxpayer – that's what happened when Sir Hans Sloane died in 1753. However, in return for the £20,000 paid by Parliament then, it received Sloane's entire collection of books, manuscripts, prints, drawings, flora, fauna and much else, which was used to found the British Museum, opened to the public today in 1759.

TILTING AT WINDMILLS

Miguel de Cervantes had his fair share of misfortune. He was shot three times while a soldier, was captured by pirates and spent five years as a slave in Algiers, and he was eventually thrown in jail for debt. But it was while in prison that he had the idea for a new kind of story – a tale with earthy characters, everyday language and plenty of adventure. His experiences gave life to *Don Quixote* (published today in 1605), one of the world's great works of literature.

MAY THE EARTH SWALLOW ME

17 A savage earthquake measuring 7.3 on the Richter Scale devastated the Japanese city of Kobe today in 1995, killing 4,600 people. Asian markets went into freefall. No joy there. But it did bring to light the antics of a financial trader who had bet megabucks that the Nikkei Index would stay above 19,000. And so the £827 million fraud run by Nick Leeson of Barings Bank came to light and the rogue trader got 6½ years in prison.

PLAYTIME

18 The production of a play about Soviet workers who go on a drink-binge didn't go as planned today in 2010. The actors decided to replace the water in their bottles with real vodka 'as an experiment'.
They proceeded to get absolutely smashed during the performance: one fell off a table, another off the stage completely, and the star was so manic the police were called. The audience, however, loved it, with many reporting the new version was more entertaining than the original text.

IT BEATS DEEP-FRIED MARS BARS ...

19 It was late 1985 and the teenager on trial at Scottish giants Glasgow Rangers was dreaming of football glory. Then disaster struck – he smashed his knee and his sporting career was over. Casting around for something else to do, the boy tried cooking. Sixteen years later, Gordon Ramsay had forgotten all about football as he picked up his third Michelin star on this day in 2001. Fans of top nosh and top strops can be very thankful for that shredded cartilage ...

LOVELY BLUBBERLY

20 Bad news for the northern bottlenose whale that took a wrong turn into the River Thames in central London today in 2006. Confused and injured after being bashed by boats, she died despite a valiant rescue attempt. However, the fact the poor creature was there at all showed how wonderfully clean the Thames has become. In 1957, pollution was so bad that the river was declared biologically dead. Now seals, otters, 125 species of fish and more than 400 species of invertebrates call it home.

A HOT LEAD

21 Staff at a warehouse in New York were gutted this morning in 2007 when they came to work and found they had been burgled. However, among the haul were GPS devices designed to help police locate snowploughs lost in drifts. Taking a chance, the police did a scan and found out that one of the dopey thieves had turned a device on to see how it worked. They made the easiest bust of their career.

SQUAD! BY THE LEFT, QUICK ... LAUGH!

22 When the first contingent of 150 Swiss Guards arrived at the Vatican today in 1506, it was bad news for any anarchic types who wanted to perform mischief on the Pope. It was also a shame for these crack troops, uprooted from their home and forced to go on duty wearing multicoloured pyjamas and a silly hat. But for everyone who has visited the Vatican in the following five centuries it was terrific news, as they are easily the funniest military outfits in the world.

LAMB TO THE (S)LAUGHTER

23 Charles Lamb was an eccentric writer who, it was said, could turn even a painful experience into a joke. When his play *Mr H.* was hissed into ruin by its first-night audience, Lamb actually joined in the booing because, he said, he was 'so damnable afraid of being taken for the author'. He then decided original drama wasn't for him and instead wrote *Tales from Shakespeare*, a fun version of the bard's plays for children. This came out today in 1807 and was an instant bestseller.

CLOUDY DAYS HAD SILVER LINING!

24 'Oops!' and 'radioactive' aren't words you want to hear together, but for physicist Henri Becquerel it meant an amazing discovery. He was exposing fluorescent minerals to sunlight to look for X-rays. His problem was a lack of sun – it was winter. So he stashed his equipment in a drawer and waited for a sunny day. Becquerel later found that the uranium rock had made an image on a photographic plate. He announced his discovery today in 1896 and became a pioneer of radioactivity.

MOST PRECIOUS PACKAGE

25 Today in 1905, a South African miner found the 3,106-carat Cullinan – the world's largest diamond. The Transvaal colony decided to give it to Edward VII, but how to get it safely back to Britain? Armed soldiers carried a package aboard a steamer, locked it into the captain's safe and set up a 24-hour guard. Asking for trouble, you might think. Luckily, the real diamond had simply been popped in the post. It arrived at Buckingham Palace a month later, showing how reliable posties can be!

MAKING MONEY IS CHILD'S PLAY

26 Coal fires look wonderful, but after a while they tend to make your wallpaper all sooty. Cleo McVicker realised this and in 1933 he concocted an odd-smelling, pliable putty that cleaned soot off brilliantly, bringing great profits for his company. But, as more people got central heating, demand fell and the company was in peril. Desperate for something to turn their fortunes around, Cleo's son Joseph realised that the cleaner could double as modelling clay. The squishy stuff was patented as Play-Doh today in 1965.

THE POSH PAGE 3

27 The National Geographic Society started out today in 1888 as a high-society travel club restricted to elite academics and wealthy patrons, and its official journal was as dull as you'd expect. Then Alexander Graham Bell took over. Blessed with a much more commercial mind, it was Bell who first used big photos to tell dramatic stories in the magazine. In 1896, the magazine published the first photograph of a bare-breasted woman and it can be no coincidence that it then became exceedingly popular.

HANGING AROUND TO BE BEHEADED

28

Bad news for Henry VIII today in 1547 – he died. However, this was an excellent turn of events for the Duke of Norfolk. He was at that very moment banged up in the Tower of London and scheduled to be executed in the morning. On hearing of the King's death, the lieutenant deferred obeying the warrant, and the stand-in powers thought it best not to kick off a new reign by executing one of the realm's greatest noblemen. Norfolk was later released and pardoned.

RAFFLES UNRUFFLED

29

After being charged with incompetence for his management of Java in 1815, the energetic young statesman Stamford Raffles was dispatched to run sleepy Bencoolen in Indonesia. Bored in this backwater, he set about looking for ways to expand British interests in the area. So today in 1819 he landed on an island off the Malay Peninsula and signed a trading treaty with the natives. It was rather a bonus to the British Empire that he did, because this humble trading post became Singapore.

THE KING IS DEAD, LONG LIVE THE KING

 Charles I was beheaded today in 1649, and just to rub things in a statue of him on horseback was ordered to be destroyed. John Rivett, a Holborn brazier, promised he'd melt it, but couldn't be bothered and simply slung it in a pit. Shoddy work. However, with the Restoration in 1660, kings were suddenly back in vogue, so everyone was chuffed when Rivett was able to dig the statue up. It now stands proudly at the top of Whitehall.

THE INSULT THAT STUCK

It all started as a bit of mild abuse. A disgruntled customer of a company that manufactured sticky tape told engineer Richard Drew to 'take this tape back to your stingy Scotch bosses and tell them to put more adhesive on it'. More amused than offended, Drew thought the word 'Scotch' was catchy, so he used it to rebrand the improved tape, which was launched by 3M today in 1930. It soon became the most widely known brand of adhesive tape in the world.

FEBRUARY

THE CANNY CASTAWAY

To paraphrase Han Solo, sailor Alexander Selkirk had 'a bad feeling about this' when travelling off the coast of South America in 1704. Fearing an imminent sinking at the hands of a psychotic captain, he asked to be set ashore on an uninhabited island. For Selkirk, the silver lining to his 4½ years' isolation was that the ship's later sinking proved him right. For fans of literature, it was his tale that inspired Daniel Defoe's wonderful *Robinson Crusoe*.

CRATE EXPECTATIONS

2 The cargo handler at JFK airport distinctly heard the crate say, 'What time is it? When are we going to leave?' He opened it and inside was 19-year-old Michael Szweu. Michael had emigrated from Australia but was desperate to return because he missed his friends. Unable to afford the £280 air fare, he decided to air-freight himself for £27 instead today in 1968. His plan had failed, but his impatience had undoubtedly stopped him from dying in an unpressurised and freezing-cold hold.

PAWS OFF MY PROGRAM

3 Ever filched a file off the internet? Congratulations! You're the kind of person who helped create the Information Age as we know it. Today in 1976, a 20-year-old computer whizz wrote an open letter condemning his programming peers for ripping off his program Altair Basic. As a result, he refused access to the source code for his Microsoft operating system. When this was later leased by IBM and computer hardware sales boomed, Microsoft had a virtual monopoly, and Bill Gates eventually became the world's richest man.

REVENGE OF THE GEEK

4 She'd given him a chance, but the geek undergrad was still spending too long mucking about on his computer. So the Harvard girl dumped her boyfriend. What a bummer. Seriously peeved, he stuck her photo on a little website he built that let students rate the hotness of girls: 'Facemash'. Today in 2004, that became Facebook, which now has a billion users. The dumped geek, Mark Zuckerberg, is worth $17.5 billion. His current girlfriend probably doesn't mind him mucking about on computers.

NO, I DON'T WANT A BLOODY SCRATCHCARD!

5 Sir Freddie Laker's Skytrain service went bust today in 1982, after suffering at the Machiavellian hands of big airlines determined to squash this threat to their profits. However, other entrepreneurs realised that people loved his idea of no-frills, cheap-as-chips flights – New York for £32.50? Yes, please! Freddie had blazed a trail and soon more people than ever before were jetting off for adventures abroad on Virgin Atlantic, easyJet and RyanAir – oh, wait, maybe this isn't such a silver lining after all.

FROM NO HOLIDAY TO NOBEL

6 In the late 1950s, new boys weren't allowed a summer holiday. Jack Kilby was the rookie, so he had to stay in the stuffy office while his seniors got out of town. He spent the long summer working on a fiendish problem in circuit design. After months of perspiration came that elusive inspiration – he had invented the integrated circuit, the basis of all modern computers, patented today in 1959. In 2000, he was finally awarded the Nobel Prize for his groundbreaking work.

HE GOT THE MESSAGE

7 New York, today in 1825, and a popular artist was painting the portrait of a distinguished European visitor when a messenger on horseback delivered a letter warning that his wife was ill. By the time he returned home to New Haven, 80 miles away, she had died and been buried. Heartbroken at her lonely suffering, the artist switched from painting to pursue a means of rapid, accurate long-distance communication. Which is how Samuel Morse came to invent the telegraph and the code that bears his name.

WE DID IT OUR WAY

8 The Hollywood Walk of Fame is one of the most recognisable tourist draws in the world, and today in 1960 the first eight brass star plaques were laid. When a committee drew up the original list of famous faces, some music executives realised the criteria were loaded towards the film industry; many great musical names would never qualify for a Hollywood star. Feeling a bit miffed at being left out, these executives decided to rectify this and promptly created the Grammy Awards.

KILT CLIPPED

9 Before today in 1727, Highlanders bombed around wrapped in a giant blanket – the 'great kilt'. But when clansmen began to work with machines the kilt's voluminous folds could easily catch in gears or get burned – it was a deathtrap. So industrialist Tom Rawlinson got a tailor to take his scissors to the traditional tartan garb, creating a smaller kilt, which only covered the body from the waist down. This might have ended centuries of tradition, but without it today's lucrative kilt industry would probably not exist.

GET YOUR FAX STRAIGHT

10 Priest Giovanni Caselli was a man of ideas, many of them radical – too radical for the church. After joining in with riots today in 1849 in Parma, he was forced into exile in Florence. With lots of spare time on his hands, Caselli tried a spot of inventing. The telegraph was just becoming popular and Caselli used his forced holiday to produce the world's first practical fax machine, the 'pantelegraph'. The first 'pantelegram' was sent from Lyons to Paris today in 1862.

COME ON, NECHO, LIGHT MY FIRE

11 Usually, an out-of-control campfire just carbonises your baked potato, so spare a thought for hunter Necho Allen back in 1790. Camped under a ledge in Pennsylvania, he woke to discover his campfire had ignited the mountain – the rocks themselves were ablaze. Pretty scary for him, but great news for chilly Americans. Allen had just discovered a massive deposit of anthracite, a very pure form of coal. Today in 1808, this was first successfully burned as a residential heating fuel by Judge Jesse Fell.

THIS JUST ISN'T WORKING OUT

12 William Pulteney was invited by George II to form a government when the previous administration resigned *en masse*. What an honour. Sadly, the new would-be Prime Minister couldn't find more than one person who wanted to serve in his cabinet, so he resigned today in 1746, a mere 48 hours after being offered the top job. On the bright side, as one satirist pointed out, he 'never transacted one rash thing and ... left as much money in the Treasury as he found in it'.

GOING UNDERGROUND

13 In 1867, the River Senne in Brussels was a turgid sewer. So, today, they began the expensive job of enclosing the stagnant river in massive brick channels. This solved the problem of the smell, and had several unexpected benefits. The job entailed clearing acres of slums, which reduced cholera outbreaks. It also created space for grand boulevards to be built. And in the 20th century, when the river was diverted around the city, the disused channels were ready-made tunnels for the Brussels metro.

A DIET TO DIE FOR

14 Fabled explorer Captain James Cook was stabbed to death today in 1799 by Hawaiian natives, putting a bit of a dampener on his voyage of exploration. But this was still a success because en route Cook had made great strides to combat scurvy. He added lemons, oranges, sauerkraut, celery and onions to his crew's diet, inspected his men's hands for dirt and insisted their quarters were ventilated. From then on, scurvy ceased to be such a scourge to sailors.

HE SHOULD HAVE DUCKED

15 RAF pilot Derek Sharp was doing 500mph in his Hawk jet when he hit a duck today in 1982. The bird smashed through the cockpit shield and into his face, knocking his left eye from its socket and filling the right with feathers, blood and other bits of duck. Sharp somehow managed to land the plane, and was rushed for emergency surgery. Not only was this successful, but doctors also took the opportunity to straighten Sharp's nose, which had been crooked since he broke it as a child.

WAY TO GO

16 Félix Faure had made a fine President of France: he had considerable charisma and enough diplomatic skill to help to revive the Franco–Russian Alliance. So, when he died aged 58 today in 1899, there seemed scant cause for celebration. However, since his fatal heart attack was brought on by the oral sex he was receiving from his 30-year-old mistress, it triumphantly confirmed France's reputation as a nation of legendary lovers.

MUSICAL METAMORPHOSIS

17 As the celebrated composer of *La Bohème* and *Tosca*, Giacomo Puccini was pretty confident when he launched his new opera at La Scala on this day in 1904. Unfortunately, the premiere was disastrous. However, this negative reaction threw Puccini into a storm of creativity – he immediately withdrew the opera and practically rewrote the whole thing, restructuring it radically. The second version brought down the house and *Madame Butterfly* went on to become one of the best-loved and most-performed operas of all time.

STARRY-EYED SURPRISE

18 In 1930, astronomers had a problem with Uranus and Neptune – they weren't orbiting as they should. So Clyde Tombaugh of Arizona's Lowell Observatory took a closer look. And today he discovered Pluto, the first new planet for 84 years. However, when Voyager 2 flew by Neptune in 1989, it found astronomers had originally miscalculated its mass, and this – not Pluto – had caused the orbital fluctuations. So Tombaugh got lucky – it was only thanks to a flawed prediction that he found Pluto in the first place.

BREAKFAST BOO-BOO BREAKTHROUGH

19 When a young Michigan lad was mixing a batch of bread dough for his brother, he accidentally left some boiled wheat sitting out for several hours, ruining the mix. In desperation, he rolled the dough anyway. When baked, the flaky, wheaty dough created a delicious crunchy snack. After swapping wheat for corn, the brothers set up a company to market it – the Battle Creek Toasted Corn Flake Company – on this day in 1906. This mouthful was soon changed in honour of their surnames: Kellogg.

I'LL HAVE THE MONEY AT THE END OF THE MONTH

20 King Christian I of Denmark and Norway was a proud father – his daughter Margaret was to marry James III, King of Scotland. However, like many other proud fathers, he was short of a bob or two for the wedding. Looking about for something suitable to pawn, he decided on the islands of Orkney and Shetland, which he pledged as security today in 1472 until the dowry was paid. Scotland never received a penny, and the islands have been theirs ever since.

CAN YOU DIG IT?

21 Commuter tempers were fraying in Mexico City today in 1978 – workers laying power cables were causing gridlock. Progress had ground to a halt because diggers had unearthed an enormous stone block slap-bang in the middle of a busy intersection. Fortunately, the 20-ton rock turned out to be a beautiful 15th-century bas-relief of the Aztec night goddess, Coyolxauqui. Even luckier, there was a museum of Aztec antiquities just 200 yards away.

NOT VERY FRIENDLY FIRE

22 A deadly efficient attack by a Heinkel He 111 bomber would usually be seen as bad news for the anti-Nazi war effort. So it was just as well that, in a case of misidentification, the two destroyers sunk in the assault near Dogger Bank today in 1940 were also German. Not exactly a happy ending, but, in those dark days, any victory against the Nazis was welcome.

A RELIGIOUS CONVICTION

23 Today in 1632, Galileo published his *Dialogue Concerning the Two Chief World Systems*, a book that repeated his outrageous claim that the earth orbits the sun. This upset Pope Urban VIII so much that Galileo was tried by the Inquisition and forced to spend the rest of his life under house arrest. Looking on the sunny side, however, it was while locked up that Galileo wrote *Two New Sciences*. This is perhaps his finest work and a brilliant summary of 30 years of discoveries in physics.

THE BOY FROM THE BLACK STUFF

24 When John Dickens was slung into prison today in 1824 for owing a baker £40, his 12-year-old son had to leave school and go to work. The boy spent ten hours a day in a rat-infested warehouse pasting labels on blacking bottles so his family could eat. The experience scarred the lad's psyche for life, but also fuelled his imagination and fired a desire to write. Young Charles would go on to become one of Britain's most popular authors.

PUMP UP DAS VOLUME

25 Beethoven started going deaf when he was 26, and it got so bad that you could have banged a kettledrum behind his head without him realising. But Ludwig was such a genius that he could still hear the music in his head, and the affliction only seemed to make him work harder. One of his final works was his majestic *Ninth Symphony* (which he finished today in 1824). At its premiere he had to be turned around to see the tumultuous applause of the audience.

HIDDEN BENEFITS

26 In 1934, the British heard a worrying rumour – Nazi Germany had a 'death-ray' that could use radio waves to destroy property and people. So radio researcher Robert Watson-Watt was asked to investigate the feasibility of this device. He quickly calculated that the fearsome death-ray was a physical impossibility. However, those same calculations suggested a further use of radio waves – the detection of enemy aircraft – and today in 1935 Watson-Watt gave a successful demonstration of what would become radar.

SWEET INSPIRATION

Who would want to live with someone who doesn't wash his hands? It was 1879 and Constantin Fahlberg, being an absent-minded scientist, didn't bother scrubbing after a day mucking around with chemicals – he just went home for his tea. Yuck! But as he was tucking into a roll he noticed it tasted particularly sweet. Fahlberg realised the taste was coming from his unwashed hands. The next day he went back to the lab and realised he had discovered saccharin.

THE DENSE DICTIONARY

For the 1934 edition of Webster's *New International Dictionary*, an entry was added: 'D or d, cont./ density'. In other words, the letter 'D' can stand for 'dense'. But the typesetters missed out the spaces, and 'Dord' was in the dictionary until today in 1939, when the error was spotted. But our rich language had been adorned with a new word, however briefly, and – who knows? – perhaps there are still people who to this day think dense people are 'a bit dord'.

MARCH

A BLINDING FLASH OF INSPIRATION

In 1811, an apprentice bookbinder attended lectures at the Royal Institution given by its famed head, Sir Humphry Davy. The young man sent a 300-page book of his lecture notes to Davy. Then Davy was temporarily blinded by an explosion in his lab and he remembered the young aspiring scientist. So today in 1813, Davy took the bookbinder, Michael Faraday, on as a secretary. Faraday went on to become one of history's all-time great scientists, discovering new compounds and inventing the dynamo, electric motor and transformer.

PICKING UP THE PIECES

2 John Spilsbury was a master at Harrow School who was having severe difficulty teaching a rather truculent geography class today in 1766. In a fit of pique he took the map of the British Isles and chopped it into pieces, telling his pupils to reassemble it or there would be real trouble. Spilsbury had not only made his point, he had also invented the jigsaw puzzle. It remained purely a teaching aid, until becoming a popular general entertainment in the early 20th century.

PIPING HOT

3 The blizzard of 1888 was so severe it nearly shut New York City down. People couldn't get enough wood and coal to keep their boilers going. However, those lucky enough to be supplied by the New York Steam Company were toasty. This company used a huge centralised boiler to pump heating steam along pipes to individual buildings. Although it had been founded today in 1882, after the big blizzard proved its worth customer numbers leaped from a few dozen to 1,800.

I'LL BE BRIEF ...

4 Today was a dreary day in Washington in 1841. Not only was it dismally wet and cold, but it also saw the longest and most boring inaugural presidential address in history. William Henry Harrison filled his speech with dry policy statements enlivened only with references to obscure Roman generals. It was nearly two hours long – and that was after extreme editing. On the bright side, Harrison never delivered another speech – he caught a terrible chill that later turned to fatal pneumonia.

IS IT ME OR IS THAT STAR GETTING BI-

5 Evidence shown by scientists today in 2010 finally proved that a massive asteroid smashed into Mexico 65 million years ago. This impact wasn't the best news for the creatures on earth at the time – the ensuing 'nuclear winter' made 60 per cent of all species extinct. On the upside, thanks to the dinosaurs going kaput, the stage was open for mammals to evolve beyond their mouse-like forms into the widely specialised species that populate the world today.

COOL-HEADED CLARENCE

6 Clarence Birdseye wanted to get married, but he didn't have the money. So he headed for the frozen wastes of Newfoundland to try his hand at fur trading. But he struggled to survive in the icy north, and had to be taught by the Inuit how to ice fish. After learning the basics, he spent years perfecting a fast-freezing method, then sold his patents for $22 million; today in 1930, the first Birds Eye frozen foods appeared in stores.

SPEAK UP, WILL YOU?

7 Everyone knows that Alexander Graham Bell invented the telephone. But what's not so well known is that he was inspired to do so by the tragedy of his mother's gradual deafness. She began to lose her hearing when he was 12 and the experience profoundly affected the young scientist. Bell's passion for curing her drove him to study acoustics, leading in turn to his development of the telephone, which he patented today in 1876.

STUCK IN A RUT

By 1935, the hard sand track at Daytona Beach that had once been so quick was badly rutted and the speed demons moved to Bonneville, taking their money with them. To replace them, today in 1936, local racer Sig Haugdahl promoted the first-ever stock-car race on the Daytona Beach Road Course. This was a disaster, costing the city $22,000, but the event had caught the public eye and eventually led to the creation of NASCAR, one of the most viewed professional sports in America.

IT'S AN ILL WIND THAT BLOWS SOMEBODY TO A NEW CONTINENT

Today in 1500, Pedro Cabral, a Portuguese merchant, led a spice-trading voyage to India. Trying to round Africa, for some reason he sailed so far west he discovered a new, jungle-clad country. He claimed it for Portugal, but didn't bother landing because he was too eager to get to India. However, his accidental discovery was worth more than spices – he had discovered Brazil, and its riches would make tiny Portugal a wealthy and powerful nation.

I THOUGHT YOU GOT THAT FROM IKEA?

10 A suburban couple in Milwaukee, in need of cash, asked an art prospector round to look at some of their furniture. Disappointment loomed when he told them their sideboard was worth precisely bugger all. 'However,' he said, 'that original Van Gogh you've got on your wall might be worth a bit.' The couple had inherited what they thought was a reproduction from a relative who had emigrated from Switzerland. *Still Life With Flowers* netted them $1.4 million at auction today in 1991.

THE DEFENCE CALLS THE PROSECUTION

11 Things were looking glum for a man charged with stealing a motorcycle today in 1948. Speaking for the prosecution was Sir Harold Cassel, one of England's leading barristers, who made a convincing case against him. Worse, the suspected thief had no lawyer of his own. However, when Cassel heard this, he offered to step up for the defence, and went on to eloquently demolish his own arguments. The man got off. The magistrate remarked that 'both counsel' had been 'most helpful'.

SING WHEN YOU'RE WINNING

12 The Dublin Welsh Male Voice Choir ran into a spot of traffic on their way to the hotly anticipated choral contest at the Arklow Music Festival today in 1978. They missed the start of the contest by 45 minutes and all looked lost until the judges pointed out that no other choirs had turned up at all. They were duly allowed to sing their entry and came a triumphant second – the judges docked them a place for their tardiness.

SOARING LIKE A (NOT VERY GOOD) EAGLE

13 Today in 1988, Michael Edwards, a plasterer from Cheltenham, came 58th out of 59 competitors in the Olympic ski jump, a full 45 metres behind the winner (the jumper he beat broke his leg). However, so endearing was 'Eddie The Eagle' with his bottle-end glasses and incurable optimism that, within a week of returning home on this day, he had earned £87,000. And from subsequent appearances in ads, speaking engagements and Finnish hit singles he earned a tidy £400,000 from his disastrous endeavour.

MUMMY, WHY'S THAT LADY GOT NO CLOTHES ON?

14 The Connaught Theatre in Worthing was the venue for a special treat for local youngsters today in 1998. Around 180 young film fans and their parents were awaiting the children's movie *Rainbow*. The first ten minutes were fine, then came the lesbian lovemaking, effing and blinding and full-frontal nudity of *The Rainbow*, D.H. Lawrence's earthy story of female sexual awakening. Highly inappropriate, but, on the plus side, several dads reported their Saturday morning had been cheered up greatly.

SHOOSH, WOMAN, I HAVE TO GO TO WORK

15 On the night before the Ides of March in 44 BC, Julius Caesar's wife had a prophetic dream and she begged her husband not to go to the Senate. Rome's dictator ignored 'er indoors and duly went to work, only to be stabbed in the back by his best mates, plunging the Republic into a series of civil wars. Ultimately, though, Caesar's heir Octavian was proclaimed as Augustus, the first emperor. His reign marked the beginning of 500 years of glory for the Roman Empire.

SELFLESS SACRIFICE

Today in 1912, a man walked out of a tent and into history. Captain Lawrence Oates was part of Scott's doomed expedition to the South Pole. Suffering badly from frostbite on the return, he knew if the team went at his pace they would all die. So he said: 'I am just going outside and may be some time,' and went out into the storm to his certain death. This heroic yet tragic act didn't save his friends, but Oates' bravery still shines bright today.

PADDY'S DAY

17

A 16-year-old lad in a coastal village was kidnapped by slavers. Taken to their wild country across the sea, he endured a harsh life. In desperation he prayed to God, and after five years he escaped and made it back home. The lad now had a mission – to preach the faith to the men who had abducted him. He did this so well that he became the Christian figurehead of the once-savage island nation. Which is how the English boy Patricius became St Patrick of Ireland.

SHAKEN, NOT STIRRED

18

During World War II, a British lieutenant commander visited a Portuguese casino. Portugal was neutral and there were several spies from enemy countries present. The young officer was cleaned out by a German agent at Chemin de Fer, but managed to turn this humbling experience to considerable profit when he used it as the central plot device in a little spy novel he completed a few years later, on this day in 1952: *Casino Royale*, the first James Bond adventure. The lieutenant was none other than Ian Fleming.

CANCER IS IT!

19 Carcinogenic chemical bromate was found in bottles of Dasani water today in 2004, forcing Coca-Cola to pull the plug on their £7 million promotion of the new product. What a PR disaster. But, on the bright side, it prevented them making an even bigger cock-up by continuing the campaign for this overpriced tap water that a marketing genius in the US thought would play well in Britain – 'Bottled spunk'. Lethal to body *and* bank balance, Dasani was pulled from shelves across Britain.

THE MAN WHO COULDN'T MISS

20 Aston Villa footballer Chris Nicholl was having a dreadful game against Leicester City today in 1976, as he scored not one but two own goals. However, so potent was his goal-scoring prowess that he also managed to bang in two at the other end, meaning that he scored all four goals in the 2–2 draw.

SLAVE TO LOVE

21 Things weren't going well for slave-trader John Newton today in 1748. He was on a ship that was being pummelled by a wild storm. But the storm changed his life. As the ship was nearly capsized by a huge wave, the non-religious Newton suddenly fell to his knees and prayed. The storm abated and Newton took it as a sign. He became a minister and composed many hymns, including the all-time favourite 'Amazing Grace'.

WEAVE MADE A MISTAKE

22 What we call tweed cloth was originally known as 'tweel', which is Scots for 'twill', from the twilled pattern. Today in 1830, a London merchant received a letter from a Hawick firm about an order of 'tweel'. He misread the handwritten word and took it to be a trade-name derived from the River Tweed, which flows through the Hawick area. He duly advertised his goods as 'Tweed', and the new name has been popular ever since.

PERKIN'S PURPLE PATCH

23 Student chemist William Perkin was trying to synthesise the expensive anti-malaria drug quinine and failing miserably. He did, however, manage to produce an artificial purple dye today in 1856, but, since this wasn't on the syllabus and his professor would have been displeased had he found out, Perkin had to experiment in his garden shed. Luckily the aniline mauve dye, which he patented aged just 18, made him a fortune and pretty much launched the synthetic chemical industry.

HANGING UP HIS SPURS

24 Devon Loch was winning the Grand National today in 1956. The jockey just had to keep going to win steeplechasing's greatest prize of all. Then, bizarrely, 50 yards from the finish, Devon Loch jumped into the air and crashed to the ground on his belly. The race was lost. Within a year the jockey also decided that was enough and left racing to try something else. He wrote his first book the next year and Dick Francis went on to author more than 40 international bestsellers.

LIFE IN A LAGOON

25 It's the 5th century and Attila's savage Huns are rampaging across northern Italy, raping, pillaging, burning villages and generally being rather unpleasant. In fact, the havoc they unleashed was so extreme that many Roman people took to a dank, desolate group of islands in a swampy lagoon. Still, they set about making the best of things – building bridges, cutting canals and reclaiming land. In other words, creating Venice – one of the most beautiful cities in the world, which tradition holds was founded today in 421 AD.

GET YOUR FREE VENICE *Tour* HERE

PAWS FOR THOUGHT

26 Today in 1995, *Time Out* named the Polar Bear in Soho as the worst pub in London. Takings shot up 60 per cent overnight. By the time staff had hung a banner outside saying 'The Worst Pub In The West End', it was so busy you couldn't get in the door.

A ROOM OF HER OWN

27 Poor Mary Mallon was quarantined today in 1915, and would stay there for the rest of her life – another 23 years. A carrier of typhoid, she was responsible for seven epidemics that killed three people. It didn't help that she insisted on working as a cook. So her incarceration was great news for the diners of New York. It was also a bonus for medical science: 'Typhoid Mary' was the first healthy typhoid carrier to be identified and her case helped improve understanding of the disease.

CRIME PAYS EVEN LESS

28 Today in 1993, Roger Morse of Winnipeg was approached by a mugger who shouted, 'Give me your wallet!' Morse did so, handing over $20. So far, so bad. Then, suddenly struck with outrage, he yelled, 'Give me my wallet back!' The mugger was so startled, he did. Only it was his, not Morse's, wallet that he returned. This contained $250.

THE ORIGINAL WEB SLINGER

29 From online shopping to kittens playing the piano, the World Wide Web has made itself an essential part of our modern society. After first proposing it today in 1989, Tim Berners-Lee later renounced all patent rights on the web – a disastrous financial move, you might think. But he realised that the Internet needed to be open to all if it was to succeed. So, while one man missed out on a personal fortune, we got the technology that today puts musical felines just a click away.

THE GOLD LINING

30 Today in 1867, Russia sold Alaska to the US for just $7.2 million, or about 2 cents per acre. That doesn't sound much, but at the time it was the Americans who had been stiffed. Alaska produced very little, was hard and expensive to defend, and Russia suspected Britain would soon pinch the property, leaving whoever owned it with nothing. And for nearly 30 years Alaska remained an unproductive backwater. Then, in 1896, gold was struck and almost overnight it became an extremely valuable property.

THAT SINKING FEELING

31 Floating is the one thing you really demand of a boat, so the Oxford crew were understandably upset when theirs proved unable to do this in today's 1912 Boat Race. Heavy waves sank them not far from the start. Plain sailing for Cambridge, you would think. However, the waters were so choppy that they were soon in the swim too. This was such a disaster that the race was rescheduled for the next day and Oxford actually won the rematch.

THE AYE HAS IT

It was a bad day for democracy when law student Frank Castelluccio walked into a polling booth in Michigan today in 1957. He saw that no one had even bothered to stand for the post of highway commissioner in the New Buffalo township election. As a protest, he decided to write his own name in the space. No one else had the same idea, so the good news for Frank was that single vote was enough to secure him a new job.

AN ELEMENTARY MISTAKE

2 Dmitri Mendeleev was the brilliant chemist who created the periodic table of elements. Alas, he wasn't quite so smart when it came to love. He divorced his first wife today in 1882 so he could marry his second, and the ensuing infamy stunted Mendeleev's career in academia. Forced to find a paying job, he joined the Bureau of Weights and Measures – and it was Mendeleev who formulated the strict Russian standards for the production of vodka stipulating it must be 40 per cent alcohol by volume.

BACK FROM THE DEAD

3 Australia's rare Leadbeater's possum was already having a hard time when horrific wildfires ripped through its habitat in 1939, so everyone knew it was curtains for the little beast. However, today in 1961, naturalist Eric Wilkinson saw the first specimen in more than 50 years. It turned out that the wildfire destruction had actually created the ideal habitat for the few surviving possums to thrive. By the 1980s, numbers were up to more than 7,500.

PINKY'S PENALTY

4 It was the deciding game of the British home international football championship between Scotland and England at Celtic Park today in 1896. Injury to a key player led England to bizarrely call up an amateur: Cuthbert 'Pinky' Burnup of Cambridge University and Old Malvernians. Hopelessly out of his league, Pinky's performance cost England the match and the championship. Happily, though, it stopped the FA relying on the old chaps network and encouraged them to pick people who could actually play the game.

AN EXPLOSION OF CREATIVITY

5 The colossal eruption of Mount Tambora in Indonesia, which started today in 1815, was the most powerful in history – the huge amount of ash it released made 1816 'the year without a summer'. All that ash did, however, make for spectacular sunsets as painted by Turner. And the 'incessant rainfall' forced some holidaymakers to stay inside their Swiss chalet for weeks. Bored, they competed to write the scariest story. Lord Byron wrote a poem, *Darkness*; John Polidori wrote *The Vampyre*; and Mary Shelley knocked out *Frankenstein*.

SLIP SLIDIN' AWAY

6 Roy Plunkett was nervous. Today in 1938, he checked the container he was using to cook up a new chlorofluorocarbon for refrigerant production and found that the valve was frozen shut and the gas had disappeared. Fearing a massive explosion, he took it outside, built a shield and cut the cylinder open. To his relief, there was no toxic boom – just a white powder that didn't stick to the container. Plunkett's snafu had created polytetrafluoroethylene – now better known as Teflon.

STRIKE A LIGHT

It was 1826 and English pharmacist John Walker was cheesed off. The stick he'd been using to stir his latest potion had stuck hard to the table. After some effort, Walker freed the stick and tried to scrape the hardened lump off the end. It burst into flames. The mixture of antimony sulphide, potassium chlorate, gum arabic and water on a stick became the first strikable match. Walker started selling them today in 1827.

DIGGING UP A CLASSIC

The Greek peasant ploughing his field on Milos today in 1820 must have felt his heart sink when his ploughshare hit a huge block of stone. He dug deeper to try to shift the thing and realised there were more, and they were actually ancient statues. He sold the find to a French archaeological team, and one of them was put in the Louvre, where it became one of the most famous works of art in history – the *Venus de Milo*.

PUTTING HIS BODY ON THE LINE

9 Things weren't going well too for Glyndwr Michael today in 1943. His biggest problem was that he was lying in a London morgue, stone dead after eating rat poison. But that wasn't the end of poor old Glyndwr – his body still had a mission to accomplish. The cunning British Intelligence dressed his corpse as a military courier with forged documents and dumped him off the coast of Spain. When found, his fake intelligence duped the German High Command into moving their Panzer tank units to Greece, rather than Sicily, which the allies promptly invaded. The charmingly named 'Operation Mincemeat' saved many thousands of British lives.

LETTING IT BE

10 Today in 1970, Paul McCartney announced that he was leaving The Beatles, which was nothing less than tragic for Fab Four fans at the time. Looking back, though, it was a brilliant move. Tensions within the band threatened the quality of their music. Splitting now meant The Beatles' legacy was untainted by substandard records. They went out at the top as the best-selling band in history. And they still had plenty of good solo tunes to come – after all, Paul was only 27.

ER ... NOTHING REALLY

11 Today in 1954 was officially the most boring day of the 20th century. Cambridge computer expert William Tunstall-Pedoe fed 300 million facts into a specially designed search engine – which used complex algorithms to link information together – and discovered there were no revolutions, no great sporting victories, just a civilised election in Belgium and the passing of ex-Oldham Athletic footballer Jack Shufflebotham. Yawn-inducing indeed. On the upside, presumably there were no earthquakes, train crashes or grisly murders either.

GOING OUT WITH A BANG

12 The invention of dynamite made Alfred Nobel a millionaire. But when his older brother died today in 1888, a French newspaper mistakenly ran an obituary of Alfred, calling him a 'merchant of death'. This shocked Nobel so much that he established the Nobel Prize in his will, offering awards to those who did most to forward the positive side of humanity in literature, peace and the sciences.

SALVATION IS AT HANDEL

13 As a young composer, George Handel enjoyed huge success with operas for the aristocracy. But he fell from vogue, and by the 1730s his health was suffering. In 1737, he had a mental and physical breakdown. But during his convalescence something remarkable happened – he completely changed his musical direction and reinvented himself. Today in 1742, the world heard his bold oratorio *Messiah* for the first time and was suitably blown away. It became one of the most-loved works in Western music.

RISING FROM THE DUST

14 Today in 1935 saw some of the US's worst 'Black Blizzards' – the catastrophic dust storms of the Dust Bowl – when ferocious winds tore away millions of pounds of topsoil from farmland. The horrors of the drought and subsequent forced migration of thousands inspired artists such as folk singer Woody Guthrie and novelist John Steinbeck. Their amazing works about these hard times also helped draw public attention to the disaster. Subsequent government action, including the planting of 200 million trees, helped halt the destruction.

A SINKING FEELING

15 What on earth could be positive about the sinking of the RMS *Titanic* today in 1912? When the largest passenger steamship in the world struck an iceberg, 1,517 people perished in the deadliest ever accident at sea. But so shocking was the tragedy that it forced through several new safety improvements, including better hull designs, easier access to lifeboats, more effective life-vests, compulsory safety drills and new radio communications laws. These went on to actually *save* lives at sea.

ALBERT'S ACID

16 A Swiss chemist named Albert Hofmann was experimenting with compounds derived from a poisonous fungus called ergot today in 1943. Unfortunately, one of the substances he was handling, lysergic acid diethylamide, got into his bloodstream through his fingertips. Hofmann soon started seeing some very strange things, and began to believe his neighbour was a witch. He was, in fact, on the world's first LSD trip. Twenty years later, the drug would help fuel the explosion of creativity and cultural change that was the 60s.

BELIEF IN ACTION

17 Martin Luther's tirades against the Catholic Church's excesses were causing uproar. Luther refused to back down today in 1521 and he was excommunicated, declared an outlaw and spent much of the rest of his life on the run. While not great for Luther, he seemed to thrive on adversity. He translated the Bible into everyday German, led the way in clerical marriage and pooh-poohed the corrupt practice of indulgences. All in all, he became the hero of the Protestant Reformation and individual conscience.

MUG SHOT

18 The Sony Centre in Cardiff was targeted by a bold thief today in 1993. Steve Driscoll was determined to pinch a camcorder. He waited until the shop was busy, selected the model he wanted and made his move. On the plus side, the model Steve had targeted was, in fact, the shop's CCTV camera. Not only was it bolted to the wall, but in his repeated attempts to grab it he kept staring straight into the lens, giving police a picture-perfect view of his face.

WAY OUT WEST

19 Mae West's play *Sex* had been on stage for a year and was doing moderately well when the NYPD decided to arrest her for obscenity. She was sentenced to 10 days in jail today in 1927. Not only did West enjoy the punishment (she dined with the warden and his wife), but it was also great publicity. Her notoriety also enabled her to launch a movie career at the age of 38. Her first film gave Cary Grant his big break and its profits saved Paramount Studios from bankruptcy.

WAIT A MINUTE, THIS IS DEFINITELY NUT CHOCOLATE!

20 The post-war period was tough for Italian patisserie owner Pietro Ferrero. Stiff taxes on cocoa beans made making chocolate goodies expensive. But, although he was short of choccy, the one thing he did have coming out of his ears was hazelnuts – the Piedmont area is famous for them. So Ferrero created a chocolate substitute from the nuts and today in 1964 the first jar of Nutella left the factory. Lucky kids all over Europe spread it on their toast and Ferrero's company became famous.

APRIL

THE COMEBACK KING

When George Bernard Shaw's *Arms and the Man* premiered at the Avenue Theatre today in 1894, the performance was well received and Shaw was invited up for a curtain call. But, before he could say a word, a solitary hiss from the gallery threatened to take the gloss off proceedings. Shaw's renowned wit came to his rescue. He bowed and said coolly, 'I quite agree with you, Sir, but what can two do against so many?' The audience erupted in delight.

DIVING INTO HISTORY

When the second mate on a Cunard ship, *Russia*, travelling from New York to Liverpool saw a man go over the side today in 1873, he instantly dived into the stormy Atlantic after him. Tragically, Matthew Webb failed to find the man, but he was still fêted as a hero and received the Stanhope Medal. The incident also gave this previously unremarkable man prodigious faith in his own swimming abilities. In August 1875, he became the first man to swim the English Channel.

BANGLE BUNGLE

23 Today in 1991, Gerald Ratner, owner of the eponymous high-street jewellery chain, stood up at an Institute of Directors dinner and famously admitted that his company's products were 'total crap'. Very bad news for Ratner – the company dropped in value by £500 million and he was later sacked. But, on the upside, his remarks at what he thought was a private bash are now used as a lesson to all to be careful how they choose their words, for fear of 'doing a Ratner'.

RAMBLING RENEGADES

24 Ramblers are usually more amiable than anarchic. But, when gamekeepers prevented them from climbing Kinder Scout, a group of irate walkers conducted a mass trespass of the Peak District hill today in 1932, with some being jailed following scuffles with gamekeepers. The ramblers' protest exposed the fact that ordinary people were denied access to much of their own country. The law moved slowly, but eventually this event led to the creation of the Peak District National Park – the UK's first – in 1951.

EDUKASHUN, EDUKASHUN, EDUKASHUN

25 The Conservatives on Derby City Council produced their new education manifesto today in 1994. Called *It's All About Standards*, it promised to be another utterly dull piece of party rhetoric. Happily, however, it contained 19 spelling, grammar and punctuation errors in just three pages. It is now a collector's item.

REDS CARE

26 Like many schoolchildren in the 1980s, Samantha Smith was terrified of nuclear war. So she wrote to Soviet leader Yuri Andropov asking him why he wanted to destroy America. To the 10-year-old's amazement, he actually wrote back today in 1983, inviting her to come and see his country for herself. Samantha flew to Moscow with her parents and spent two weeks as Andropov's guest. She was amazed by the friendliness of the people and the incident was a great boost for US–Soviet relations.

CUPPA CHAOS

27 The Tea Act sounds about as threatening as a piece of shortbread, but, when Parliament passed it today in 1773, it started a very disastrous chain of events. The Act gave the British East India Company a monopoly on the North American tea trade; understandably, the colonists objected. In December, their resistance culminated in the Boston Tea Party and within two years the American War of Independence had broken out. Bad news for Britain, but without the Tea Act the United States might not have been born.

BLIGH'S BOUNTY

28 Today in 1789 could have started better for William Bligh: he woke to see his crew pointing bayonets at him. They were taking over his ship, the *Bounty*, so they could return to Tahiti, whose women were far more appealing than a Pacific crossing on a weevil-infested boat. So Bligh was cast adrift, while his men returned to paradise. However, Bligh brilliantly sailed the tiny boat 6,701 km to Timor, and the amazing tale has inspired countless plays, poems, books and films to this day.

WHAT A GRAPE IDEA

29 In 1872, a deadly mildew infested many of France's finest vineyards. Production plummeted and growers were ruined. Botanist Pierre-Marie-Alexis Millardet, desperately searching for a remedy, noticed that farmers in the Medoc painted something called 'Bordeaux mixture' on their vines to stop theft. This concoction was so foul-tasting it did indeed deter thieves – and the harmful mildew. It enabled Millardet to isolate the world's first fungicide. He published his findings today in 1885 and soon corks were flying all over France in celebration.

I'LL PUT UP WITH THIS MISTAKE

In 1968, a scientist at 3M named Spencer Silver developed a new type of glue – it was strong enough to hold pieces of paper together, but it could easily be pulled apart again. 'Completely unmarketable,' was the judgement of his stuck-up bosses. Years later a colleague complained that the snippets of paper he used to mark his hymn books kept falling out. Spencer saw the light and his 'failed project' was launched to the world as the Post-it Note today in 1980.

MAY

THE POX THAT MADE THE POTTER

As a little boy, Josiah Wedgwood was a skilled potter, but when smallpox disabled his knee he was unable to work the foot pedal of a potter's wheel. So he concentrated more on designing pottery and experimenting with new production techniques. At this he was not just skilled, but absolutely brilliant, and he invented many new pottery styles on his way to becoming the most famous potter of all time. Today in 1759, he founded the Wedgwood company.

ARE YOU SURE THIS IS THE WAY TO WINDERMERE?

2 Next time you use your satnav, spare a thought for Korean Air Lines Flight 007, shot down in 1983 with the loss of 269 lives after accidentally straying into USSR airspace. To prevent a recurrence of the tragedy, President Reagan sanctioned the development of a satellite location system – then planned only for US military purposes – for civilian use. So over the next 20 years the US built, launched and activated 24 new satellites. And today in 2000, President Clinton finally made accurate GPS services available to everyone.

THE BYRONIC MAN

3 Lord Byron spent his life being a maverick in as many ways as he could – as a poet, lover, rake and freedom fighter – but a deformed right foot prevented him excelling physically. Until he turned to a long-neglected athletic arena – swimming. His foot mattered less in the water, and his open-water swims are the first of modern times. He had aquatic adventures in Cambridge, Venice, Lisbon and, today in 1810, the disabled aristocratic poet became the first person in recorded history to swim the Hellespont, Turkey.

SPIRIT OF INVENTION

Increasing competition from the USA and Germany was destroying Fred Royce's engineering business. In near desperation he cast around for something else to make, and eventually tried building one of the new-fangled 'motor cars'. He showed his first effort to a business associate, who introduced him to Charles Rolls, owner of a London car showroom. Rolls and Royce met for the first time today in 1904 and were soon making some of the finest cars in the world.

CINQ YOU, SISTER

In 1895, a young French girl called Gabrielle lost her dear *maman* to tuberculosis and was placed in a convent for orphans. Life was fiercely strict and the order was big on numerology. The nuns particularly liked the number 5 – it signified the pure spirit of a thing. The convent always stayed with Gabrielle, and when she launched a revolutionary perfume today in 1921 she named it simply with her surname and that mystic number – 'Chanel No. 5'. It became the most famous scent in the world.

(I CAN'T GET NO) SOMNAMBULATION

6 A young rock'n'roll guitarist checked into a Florida hotel today in 1965, had a little 'refreshment' and passed out on his bed. When he woke up, he felt awful, but he noticed that his guitar and tape recorder were by his side. He rewound the tape and pressed play, and out rocked a completely new riff – which he had apparently recorded at some point in the night – followed by 40 minutes of snoring. The riff became the song 'Satisfaction', the Rolling Stones' biggest hit.

A BURNING SENSE OF INJUSTICE

7 When Ludger Sylbaris was thrown in jail for fighting in a St Pierre bar on the Caribbean island of Martinique today in 1902, he probably thought he'd been pretty hard done by. He was locked in a windowless, stone-walled underground cell. The next morning, however, the nearby volcano, Mount Pelée, decided to erupt. This was disastrous for the people in St Pierre – 30,000 of them were killed. Ludger, however, was protected by his cell and was one of only two survivors. He was later pardoned.

THE FIZZY PHARMACEUTICAL

8 Back in 1885, Atlanta pharmacist John Pemberton spent ages perfecting what he thought was an effective new headache medicine – Pemberton's French Wine Coca. However, local temperance officials forced him to reformulate it without the booze. They also pointed out that it was useless as a painkiller. However, they did admit that it tasted great. So, with a couple of little tweaks to the recipe and some carbonated water, Pemberton relaunched it today in 1886 as a soft drink instead – Coca-Cola.

BRANDY FOR HEROES – AND HEARTS

9 In the 14th century, transporting heavy wine casks was a real pain, not to mention being expensive. So merchants began to distil it before shipping, then added back the water before consumption. Drinkers decided, though, that the stronger drink was a heart-warming improvement. Today in 2007, scientists announced that drinking Armagnac – the oldest brandy in France – might explain why the people of Gascony have one of the lowest rates of cardiovascular disease in the world.

HIS CAREER IS LOOKING UP

10 Back in the early 16th century, a man fell out with his boss, who wanted to take him off his current job and give him a new task. The dude refused – he felt the other type of work wasn't really his thing and that it would take too long. His boss, Pope Julius II, pulled rank and ordered him to get to work on this day in 1508. And so the world's greatest decorator, Michelangelo, reluctantly set about painting the ceiling of the almighty Sistine Chapel. The world has stared in wonder every day since.

YOUR NAME'S NOT DOWN

11 Security guard Carl Shimmin didn't want to turn away the nice 'old dear' driving a Vauxhall Carlton from the Royal Windsor Horse Show today in 1991, but she didn't have a sticker on her window, and rules are rules. However, the lady asked him to check. Carl wasn't sure, but luckily for him he decided to ask a colleague, who pointed out that the old dear was Elizabeth, the Queen of England. Her Majesty had decided to drive herself the 500 yards from Windsor Castle to the show. Carl let her in, stickerless.

SCUPPERED IN SCAPA

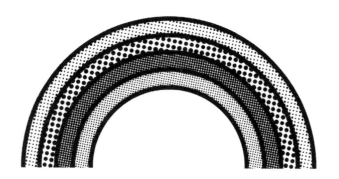

After a German U-boat got into Scapa Flow and torpedoed HMS *Royal Oak* in 1939, killing 833 men, Churchill ordered the construction of a series of massive barriers to block the eastern entries to the Orkney harbour. This was such a huge construction job that the barriers weren't finished until this day in 1945 – four days after the war in Europe ended. However, they didn't go to waste – they made perfect causeways and now handily carry the A961 road from Kirkwall to Burwick.

BOLDLY GOING WHERE NO ONE WANTED TO GO BEFORE

13 Eleven ships full of 696 convicts, 212 marines and their families, and 81 'free persons' left Portsmouth today in 1787. The journey they embarked on was a horrendous one: for 15,000 miles they were crammed together in foul and disease-ridden conditions; 48 people died on the way. The good news was that when they finally did arrive, 252 days after setting off, they had practically a whole sunny continent to themselves. They were the 'First Fleet' that became the original European settlers in Australia.

FULL STEAM AHEAD

14 When the Bryn Eglwys slate quarry closed in 1946, it looked like the Talyllyn Railway that served it would die too. However, the little trains that twisted through the Welsh mountains had a lot of big fans and they came together to save it from the axe. Today in 1951, it became the first railway in the world to be operated by volunteers. The Rev. W. Awdry wrote several stories based on the Talyllyn Railway and the line also inspired the film *The Titfield Thunderbolt*.

VEGAS IS THE BOMB

15 Las Vegas, founded today back in 1905, was a two-bit railroad town for years and still a small city after World War II. Then, in 1951, the US military detonated a nuclear bomb in the desert nearby and Vegas exploded too. Scientists from the testing range came for some non-plutonic fun with the locals, visitors admired mushroom clouds from their balconies, and hotels posted bomb test-times. It's only thanks to the most destructive weapon in history that the party city exists as it is.

PARK LIFE (AND DEATH)

16 In medieval times, powerful landowners sealed off huge areas of the country for their own hunting pleasure. This was pretty rough on the local starving peasants – they'd be hanged if caught with so much as a bunny up their bodkin. However, as cities grew in later centuries, these selfishly preserved green spaces often became the parks that we now enjoy our sandwiches in. London's Richmond Park opened to the public today in 1758, after a local brewer sued the royal household and demanded public access.

THE WRONG GUY

17 Guy Goma had gone to the BBC for an interview as a data-inputter. He was surprised, therefore, to find himself being interviewed live on TV about Internet litigation. Perhaps thinking this was some arcane BBC initiative test, Guy did his best, but his dithering answers soon made producers realise there had been a case of mistaken identity. Hugely embarrassing for the BBC, and poor Guy didn't even get the job. On the bright side, it did put a smile on a lot of faces.

GOLFERS DRIVEN OFF

18 Today in 1491, King James IV of Scotland banned golf (and football) because they were distracting the nation's men from archery practice. But, like much prohibition, the law had the opposite effect – it simply drew people's attention to these sports, which consequently flourished. Fifty years later, golf was even a royal game – Mary Queen of Scots could often be seen on the links swishing her mashie.

SUFFERING FOR HIS ART

19 Unrequited love for a fellow student caused Alfred Housman to have a breakdown. He failed his final exams at Oxford, handing in papers that were blank or covered in random scribbles. His thwarted passion eventually drove him to become a recluse. He poured his heartache into his poetry and, today in 1896, he self-published his collection *A Shropshire Lad*. This was hailed as a masterpiece and A.E. Housman became one of England's most-loved and oft-quoted poets.

ENCOURAGE THE OTHERS

20 Admiral John Byng was a distinguished Royal Navy officer who, through his cautious action at Minorca today in 1756, allowed the island to fall to the French. History suggests he acted prudently, but he was nevertheless court-martialled, found guilty of failing to 'do his utmost' and shot by firing squad. Looking back, this does seem a little harsh. But it helped inculcate an aggressive and determined mindset in British officers, giving the Royal Navy a vital edge over their international rivals.

I'VE ONLY HAD A FEW ALES

21 Today in 1983, 40-year-old Peter Woodend was nursing the daddy of all hangovers. Found blacked-out and naked outside a hospital, his blood-alcohol level was an incredible 1,010 mg – 13 times the legal limit and the highest ever recorded. Just 300 mg can be fatal and no one usually survives 600 mg, let alone nearly double that. So, while his hangover undoubtedly was a belter, he could take some solace from the fact that he was a record breaker! Now that's dedication …

WHO GIVES A PUCK?

22 A new type of maze-based video game was released in Japan today in 1980. But when the manufacturers tried to sell it to American company Midway, there was a problem. Midway refused to release a game called 'Puck Man'; they knew full well that kids would vandalise the letter 'P' … So, the name was changed, and the catchily titled 'Pac-Man' became the highest-grossing video game of all time.

THIS IS AN EX-IDEA

23 When the Monty Python team first got together, they decided to not 'cap' their unusual and innovative sketches in the traditional manner. Then their hearts sank as they saw Spike Milligan take the same approach in his groundbreaking series *Q5*. Forced to come up with something original as well as anarchic, they decided to blend sketches into one another in a single stream-of-consciousness. And, today in 1969, the BBC approved their first series and the revolutionary comedy team's place in TV history was assured.

I'D LIKE TO TEACH THE BAND TO SING

24 Usually it's the Norwegians who fail this miserably at Eurovision. But, today in 2003, it was Britain's turn. Our entry 'Cry Baby' by Jemini was so off-key it did indeed bring tears to the eyes. It was – quite justly – awarded 'nul points'. However, there was an upside. Thanks to all the exposure that the contest gave Jemini, the song actually became a modest hit, reaching No. 15 in the UK singles chart.

WHAT THE FALK?

25 The Falklands War was at a crucial stage and the Parachute Regiment were ready to make a top-secret attack on Darwin and Goose Green. Then their commander heard a BBC World Service newsreader announce the planned raid. Argentine forces were also listening to the broadcast. However, since the Argies took the understandable view that no country would announce its battle plans to the enemy, they dismissed it as a crude bluff. The assault went ahead and was a British success.

BLOODY BRILLIANT

26 In the 1450s the ruler of Wallachia, a principality in modern Romania, was carving out a fearsome reputation for cruelty. Unfaithful lovers were skinned alive, visiting ambassadors who refused to remove their hats had them nailed to their head, and he is rumoured to have impaled thousands of people on stakes, often drinking their blood. Pretty grim all round, really, but this demonic man became the inspiration for one of the most popular characters in literature – Dracula. Bram Stoker published his dark tale today in 1897.

HARD EVIDENCE

27 The American pharmaceutical company, Pfizer, had a new drug that was meant to help high blood pressure and relieve angina. Only it wasn't helping at all. All it did was give patients erections. A diverting side effect, but hardly useful ... oh, *wait* a minute. So the researchers launched a new clinical trial, this time using the drug to combat erectile dysfunction. They waited 15 minutes and ... *ooh la la*! And so Viagra first raised its head today in 1998. Within a year, it was raking in $1 billion in sales.

WANTED

UNDEAD ⅌ ALIVE

PRINCE VLAD

PAYMENT ᴵᴺ SILVER

I HAVE IN MY HAND A
HOLIDAY REQUEST FORM

Neville Chamberlain became Prime Minister today in 1937 and pretty much everyone agrees that that had a whopper of a downside – his lame strategy of appeasement towards Hitler helped bring about World War II. However, if he hadn't been elected, he wouldn't have been able to enact one of his pet pieces of legislation – the Holidays with Pay Act. And you wouldn't be able to enjoy paid holiday from work.

WHAT GOES UP MUST GO UP AGAIN

Swiss climber Raymond Lambert was a tough nut. Despite having previously lost all his toes to frostbite, in 1952, he got to within 237 metres of the top of Everest. Alas, poor planning and basic equipment meant that he and a Sherpa were forced back down the mountain with their dream in tatters. However, the same Sherpa, Tenzing Norgay, was able to use his experience of the failure just a year later to help Edmund Hillary make it to the top of the world on this day.

WRECKED IN RETREAT

30 The Spanish Armada, which sailed out of Lisbon today in 1588 on its mission to invade England, carried a huge army led by a brilliant general. But, when English fire ships scattered some Spanish vessels, he made a crucial decision – to head north round Scotland. The Armada was devastated by fierce storms and disease in the harsh northern waters, and Spain's chance to conquer England was gone. On the bright side, if they'd succeeded, they'd only have spent all their time moaning about our lousy weather …

DEAREST DIARY

31 Samuel Pepys' diary is a famous account of 10 years of the English Restoration period (1660–69). But, towards the end of the decade, Pepys' eyesight worsened. Fearful that he was going blind from too much writing, though still only 36, he ended his diary today in 1669 and had the whole thing bound for posterity. If he hadn't it would probably have been lost among his many papers but, as it was, he bequeathed it to Magdalene College, where its treasures were rediscovered 150 years later.

JUNE

HE WAS A DEAD GOOD POLITICIAN

1 Today in 2008, the mayor of Voinesti in Romania, Neculai Ivascu, died on election day. Bad news for him, but also for the townspeople who felt he had been a rather good mayor. However, they weren't the sort of people to let a mere thing like death stand in the way of good governance, so they simply re-elected him anyway. He beat the living candidate by 37 votes.

WHERE TO, YER 'IGHNESS?

It was the coronation of Queen Elizabeth II today in 1953 and tradition decreed that each Commonwealth Prime Minister have his own horse-drawn carriage for the journey to Westminster Abbey. There was just one problem – professional coachmen were a bit thin on the ground these days. Luckily, a group of businessmen and country squires offered their driving services. They dressed as Buckingham Palace servants to fool the crowds and made it to the church on time, bagging a front-seat view into the bargain.

FAILURE OF THE FLY-BOY

It was 1940 and German Panzer divisions had cut British forces off from the retreating French and pushed them back to Dunkirk, the last continental channel port in Allied hands. Then, bizarrely, the Panzers were ordered to halt. Herman Goering wanted his Luftwaffe to have the glory of finishing off the British. However, bad weather prevented this, and by today 338,000 men had been evacuated. Not only was this a triumph for British morale, but also the men were free to be deployed elsewhere.

FROMAGE NOT VERY FRAIS

4 A French shepherd tending his flocks sheltered in a cave and accidentally left his lunch behind when he went off after a passing mademoiselle. Returning weeks later (she was that kind of girl), his cheese had started to rot, being thick with blue veins and smelling fairly rank. Yuck. But he scoffed the lot, decreed it delicious and so Roquefort was born. Charles VI gave the nearby town a monopoly on production today in 1411.

ROMANCE ON RAILS

5 In the 19th century, a young Belgian engineer called Georges, rejected by the love of his life, went to the United States to forget her. There he spent 10 months exploring the country by train. Georges returned to Europe intoxicated by the romance of such long, luxurious journeys. He later founded the Compagnie Internationale des Wagons-Lits, which today in 1883 ran a new service from Paris to Vienna. This was later extended to Istanbul and became known as the 'Orient Express'.

THE RHYTHM OF HIS HEART

6 American engineer Wilson Greatbatch was making a circuit to help record fast heart sounds. Unfortunately, he used the wrong resistor. The circuit he created was a total failure as a recording device: it pulsed for 1.8 milliseconds, stopped for one second, and then repeated this rhythm endlessly. Greatbatch suddenly realised that the sound resembled a perfect heartbeat. Today in 1960, the device was implanted into a 77-year-old man with an irregular heartbeat. Those clumsy fingers had helped create the first practical pacemaker.

THE SWEET SMELL OF SUCCESS

7 The summer of 1858 was so hot in London that it created the 'Great Stink'. The hum from the raw sewage flowing into the Thames was so humungous that Parliament was suspended today. This thankfully kick-started MPs into action and over the next six years 550 miles of main sewers and 13,000 miles of local sewers were built. This was an expensive way to get rid of a smell, but there was a bonus. Removing the sewage also got rid of London's regular cholera outbreaks.

ORWELL UNWELL

8 Getting tuberculosis is bad enough, but when you're living in the sooty, dirty heart of London it's even worse. So George Orwell decided to clear out to a healthier place, settling in a remote farmhouse on the Scottish island of Jura. Orwell connected instantly with the bleakly beautiful landscape and it was here that he found the peace and time to write his final masterpiece, *1984*, published today in 1949. By 1989, it had been translated into 65 languages, the greatest number for any English-language novel.

FROM BAD TO VERSE

9 When unemployed weaver William McGonagall decided to become a poet today in 1877, it was a bad day for lovers of quality verse. McGonagall was easily the worst poet the world has ever known. But if he'd been a slightly better poet – just bad rather than truly awful – he wouldn't have found work reading his gems in the circus, where the audience could get their thrills pelting him with eggs, flour, herrings, stale bread and potatoes.

A VOTE FOR ELECTORAL REFORM

10 We all know politics is boring, but the council election at Pillsbury in North Dakota today in 2008 set a record for lack of voter interest. For the first time in the history of democracy, no one at all cast a ballot, not even the six standing candidates. So, despite being utterly unopposed, no candidate was elected. Happily, however, the county auditor pointed out that the councillors would now have to appoint *someone* to do their jobs. They duly appointed themselves.

I DEDUCE I SHOULD TRY ANOTHER CAREER

11 Proudly, the 23-year-old doctor opened the door of his new Southsea practice today in 1882. He had just taken a bold risk, using his last £10 to start his career. But customers did not come through the door, and soon it was his business that was sick. But, rather than get disheartened, the resourceful young MD used the down-time to scribble a few short stories. Soon Dr Arthur Conan Doyle's bank account would be very healthy – he had just created Sherlock Holmes.

DEAR DIARY

12 Today in 1942, a Dutch girl received a diary for her thirteenth birthday. A month later, she was forced to go into hiding from the Nazis, who were rounding up all Jews. Discovered after two years, she died of typhus in the Bergen-Belsen concentration camp in March 1945. Her diary, however, survived. Beautifully written, it details not only the poignant coming-of-age feelings of a teenage girl, but is also a document of human fortitude in the face of one of history's most tragic events. *The Diary of Anne Frank* is one of the world's most widely read books.

FINANCIAL INDEPENDENCE DAY

13 A man was browsing at a flea market in Pennsylvania, when a wooden-framed picture caught his eye. He paid $4 for it. But back home, regretting his purchase already, he changed his mind about the painting and decided to keep only the frame. So he removed the picture – and found a folded document behind it. This was a 1776 copy of the Declaration of Independence, one of only 24 known to remain. Today in 1991, he sold it at auction for a whopping $2.4m.

THE CANNY CLERGYMAN

14 Scottish settlers who moved to Kentucky in the 18th century liked the area well enough apart from one thing – they didn't have much luck growing barley. Other grains thrived, but they were upset because you needed barley to make whisky … or did you? Not according to the Reverend Elijah Craig of Bourbon County, who, today in 1789, produced the first whiskey distilled from maize. Markedly different in taste, 'bourbon' did the job of getting you drunk just as well as Scotch.

INSPIRATION STRIKES

15 In 1746, inventor Benjamin Franklin was experimenting with electricity when he gave himself a massive shock that sent him into spasms and made his head go numb. Normal people would have walked away at this point, but Franklin was just getting started. Today in 1752, he tied a key to a kite and took it for a jaunt into a storm. This potentially suicidal stunt finally proved that lightning is electricity, and Franklin's lightning rods were soon protecting spires and other tall buildings from damage.

SUCCESS IS RELATIVE

16 Having failed his dissertation and been unable to get a university post, the young Albert Einstein was forced to take a job as a clerk in the Swiss Patent Office in Bern, today in 1902. This turned out to be a blessing in disguise. He found the work stimulating, the pay was good, and he had time to think about physics. He was soon publishing scientific papers and within three years had come up with his special theory of relativity.

A LOVE EVERLASTING

17 Today in 1631, a woman called Mumtaz Mahal died during childbirth. Her husband was so distraught he resolved to put up a monument befitting her memory. And since he was the fabulously wealthy Mughal emperor Shah Jahan, he could think a little grander than a park bench. For 17 years, the finest craftsmen laboured beside the Yamuna River building a marble mausoleum for Mumtaz. The result was the Taj Mahal, one of the most beautiful buildings the world has ever seen.

BRUMMIE BUTTON BRAVERY

18 A travelling button salesman was in Brussels today in 1815 when he stumbled upon the Battle of Waterloo. The Duke of Wellington himself spotted the civilian and called him over, warning him he was in danger of his life. 'Not more than your Grace,' he replied. Perhaps calling his bluff, the great Duke asked him to deliver a battle order, which the man did. Wellington later rewarded the unflusterable rep with a position in the Royal Mint.

WHO'S LAUGHING NOW?

19 A young cartoonist called Jim Davis created a strip called Gnorm Gnat, which he offered to newspaper editors, without success. One told him, 'Your art is good, your gags are great, but bugs – nobody can relate to bugs!' He went back to the drawing board (literally), creating the cuddliest character he could think of – a fat, lazy, marmalade cat. *Garfield* debuted today in 1978 and quickly became the fastest-selling comic strip in the world. Today it is read by an estimated 263 million people every single day.

WHO CAN THAT BE AT THIS TIME?

20 Cold War tensions nearly erupted into worldwide nuclear conflict during the Cuban Missile Crisis in 1962. Nerves were particularly frayed during the 12 hours it took the US to receive and decode a crucial 3,000-word message from Nikita Khrushchev. So, today in 1963, the US and USSR installed the nuclear 'Hot Line', directly linking Washington and Moscow. As well as looking very cool in films, the red phone was soon put into use, helping to calm tensions during various conflicts around the globe.

RADIO GA GA

21 Today in 1998, zany breakfast DJ Phil Holmes of Sunderland's Sun FM dozed off around 7 a.m. and remained asleep at his mic for half an hour. A standby system cut in and automatically played soothing records until furious bosses woke him up. They later fired him. On the bright side, regular listeners reported that they had hugely enjoyed the show. The peaceful interlude made a happy change from the usual cacophony of bad jokes, cheesy sound-effects and annoying phone-ins that constitute breakfast radio.

THE BIGGEST BAD IDEA EVER

When Operation Barbarossa – Hitler's invasion of the Soviet Union – began today in 1941, things looked bleak for Russia, and they were hit by 150,000 casualties in the first week. But by drawing Hitler into Russia until his forces were overstretched, and through heroic defence at places like Stalingrad and Leningrad, Stalin eventually inflicted a humiliating defeat on Hitler, and it marked a turning point in World War II.

ON YOUR MARKS, GET SET, FIGHT!

In 1892, the mind of French Baron Pierre de Coubertin was on war. He was worried that his puny, waif-like countrymen were no physical match for neighbouring macho-men Germany – he feared they'd be trounced if war was to ever broke out. Looking for a way to improve French fitness, the Baron proposed reviving the ancient Olympic ideal. And so from one Frenchman's bellicose paranoia the modern Olympics – an event watched by the billions – were reborn today in 1894.

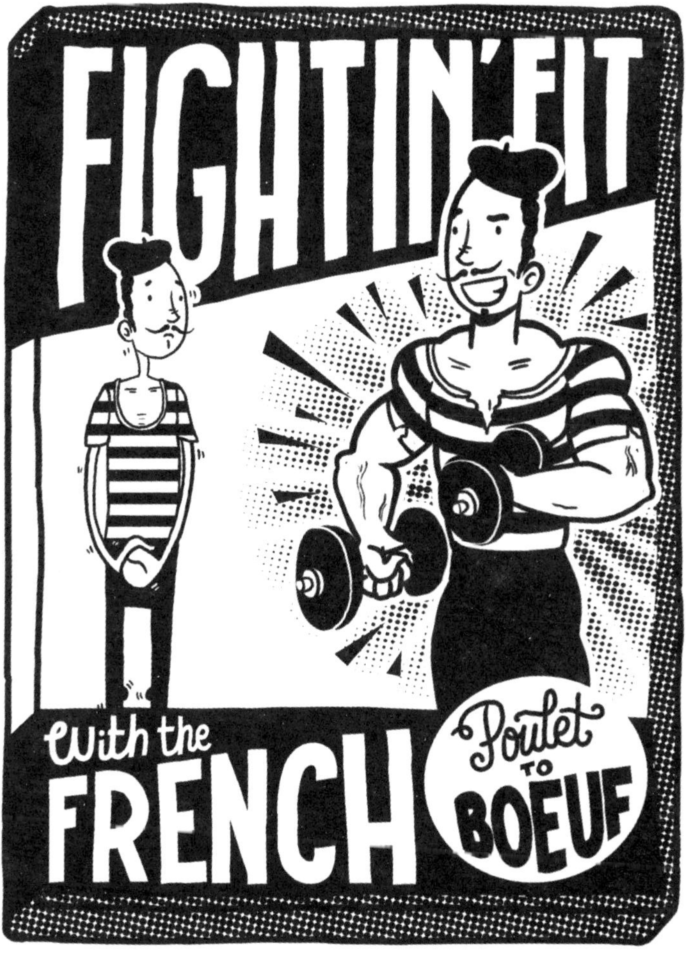
FIGHTIN' FIT
with the
FRENCH
Poulet
TO
BOEUF

ONE GOOD YEAR, MANY BAD ONES

24 Convinced he could formulate a rubber compound that didn't melt when the sun came out, an inventor lost the plot. He was thrown in jail three times, lost thousands of dollars in a financial crash and was facing poverty. He was literally shaking his fist in rage at another failure when the mixture flew from his hand onto a hot stove. Inspecting the charred remains, he realised that it had hardened into a usable form. Today in 1844, Charles Goodyear received his patent for vulcanised rubber.

BULLETPROOF BRILLIANCE

25 Thousands of police officers and soldiers around the world can be very glad that Stephanie Kwolek ran out of money in 1946. Without the cash necessary to study medicine as she wanted, she took a research position with DuPont's textile fibres lab instead. It turned out she was a naturally brilliant chemist, her most notable achievement being the invention of poly-paraphenylene terephtalamide (patented today in 1974). Five times stronger than steel, it's light, doesn't corrode and is better known as Kevlar.

THE NATIVES ARE RESTLESS

26 Captain George Custer had always wanted fame, and, when he led the US 7th Cavalry to meet Native American warriors at the Battle of the Little Big Horn today in 1876, he thought he'd get it: Custer was convinced he'd be facing a laughably small enemy force. He was wrong – thousands of Sioux showed up. Still, Custer earned the place in history he so desired, albeit for being an arrogant idiot who got himself and his entire company killed.

NICE LEGS, SHAME ABOUT THE ACE

27 Henry 'Bunny' Austin was that rarest of all sportsmen, a good British tennis player. He made the quarter-finals or better ten times and was in two finals. But, try as he might, Bunny just wasn't *quite* good enough to win the thing. Thinking the answer must be in the restricting cricket flannels everyone wore then, Bunny became the first player to wear shorts at Wimbledon when he stepped out today in 1932. He still didn't win, but he had started a trend.

I'M FREE

28 Heavy-handed police raids on gay pubs in New York City were common in the 1960s. They went a little too far today in 1969 when they harassed punters at the Stonewall Inn in Greenwich Village. A huge crowd gathered to see cops beating drinkers and hauling them away in handcuffs, and a riot erupted. After the dust had settled, the gay community got organised for the first time and Stonewall marked the start of the gay rights movement in the United States and around the world.

ABOUT BLOODY TIME

29 When Aztec leader Montezuma welcomed Hernán Cortés and his men into Tenochtitlan and showered them with gifts, it was very bad news for the Aztecs. Within months, Cortés had massacred the Aztec aristocracy, Montezuma had been stoned to death (today in 1520) and the Aztec empire was finished. Sounds a bit harsh, but it was terrific news for the dozens of other tribes that the Aztecs had spent years sacrificing. They once sacrificed 84,400 prisoners over four days and, thankfully, all that nonsense now came to an end.

PLEASE PRESS '1' TO DIE IN SCREAMING AGONY

30 Tragedy struck in London's Wimpole Street in 1935 when a raging house fire killed five women. Worse, a neighbour had rung the fire brigade to alert them but had been put in a queue by the Welbeck telephone exchange. The subsequent publicity prompted a government inquiry and the introduction of the world's first emergency call service on this day in 1937. The 9-9-9 format was chosen because 9 was right beside the dial stop and so was easy to find even in dense smoke.

NOW I'M A BELIEVER

The congregation in the First Baptist Church in Forest, Ohio, got a fearful shock today in 2003 when a mighty lightning bolt blasted the steeple, blowing the sound system, setting the church on fire and causing $20,000 of damage. However, for the Reverend Don Hardman, who was preaching at the time, it was something of a triumph. Seconds before he had been sermonising on the topic 'God Speaks In Thunder', had raised his eyes to the heavens and asked for a sign from God.

DIGGING DEEPER

2 US President James Garfield was shot today in 1881. His assailant's bullet didn't kill him, but lodged in his body, leaving him agonisingly near death for weeks. Desperate to save the president, Alexander Graham Bell, of telephone fame, promptly invented the metal detector. His machine worked in tests but the pig-headed surgeons refused to move Garfield from his metal-sprung bed, and Bell couldn't find the bullet. The president soon died, but at least his plight had made treasure hunting easier.

HERE LIES
PRESIDENT
JAMES
GARFIELD

I LOVE YOU, DADDY ... ER, MUMMY

3 Thomas and Nancy Beatie were distraught because doctors discovered Nancy was infertile. Then Thomas pointed out that he had actually been born a woman – and despite going through the gender reassignment his female reproductive organs were still in tip-top condition, so maybe he should have a shot instead. And today in 2008, Thomas Beatie announced that he had given birth to a girl called Susan, making him the first legally male person to do so.

ALICE STAMPS HER FOOT

4 This day in 1862 was a scorcher and the Reverend Charles Dodgson was struggling to entertain a friend's children. They were hot, bored and bolshy, and 10-year-old Alice was demanding a story. And so, in desperation, he started to spin his tale. The girls loved it, and Alice begged him to write it down for her. He did, and three years later he published it and *Alice in Wonderland* became one of the best-loved children's stories of all time.

TOM'S TOURS TAKE OFF

5 Young Tom Cook was waiting for a stagecoach on the London Road to take him on a holiday – the coach was late and he was pretty fed up. It occurred to him that the best way to enjoy an excursion would be for someone else to sort it out for you. So, today in 1841, he block-booked some railway tickets, laid on some food and successfully organised an outing for 540 temperance campaigners. Within a few years, Thomas Cook's pioneering travel agency was operating all over the world.

MAD DOGS AND FRENCHMEN

When nine-year-old Joseph Meister poked a rabid dog with a stick on this day in 1885, the dog duly savaged the boy, infecting him with the disease, and his family feared the worst. However, a scientist – not a doctor – who lived nearby proposed a new treatment. The family was sceptical, but, with nothing to lose, they let him try. Happily, Joseph recovered and the unlicensed doctor – Louis Pasteur – was hailed as a hero. His success laid the foundations for the manufacture of many other vaccines.

A HOLE IN 121

Barrow's Maurice Flitcroft fancied playing in the Open golf championship that started today in 1976. He'd never played golf before, but that seemed a minor detail. He tricked his way into the qualifying round and recorded the worst ever score in the tournament's history – 121 strokes. However, his story proved an inspiration for many happy hackers and won him a free golfing holiday, courtesy of the Blythfield Country Club in Grand Rapids, who also named a tournament in his honour.

THE IDEA THAT WOOD CHANGE THE WORLD

8 The growth of printing in Europe meant demand for paper had never been higher. But paper was then made from rags, which had a very limited supply, and the shortage was threatening to halt the explosion of ideas that printing had enabled. Frenchman René-Antoine Ferchault de Réaumur was walking in the woods today in 1719 when he noticed how wasps had made a paper-like nest by chewing wood fibres – and the penny dropped. Soon paper was being made from wood pulp and the future of trivia books was assured.

AND SO TO BED

9 The Queen woke tonight in 1982 to see intruder Michael Fagan sitting on the end of her bed. Her Majesty pressed an alarm, but the guard had just gone off duty. So she coolly chatted to Fagan for 10 minutes until help came. What this showed was how easy it was to get into Buck House – he had simply scaled the Palace's wall, shimmied up a drainpipe and entered through an open window. Security improved considerably after that …

BIT OF A BREW-HA-HA

10 Where would we be without our morning coffee hit? Still in bed, probably. So it's worth thanking Pope Clement VIII who in 1600 was called on to ban the new drink from the East. His priests claimed it was a satanic potion concocted by Islamic infidels and begged Clement to ban it. Clement tasted it for himself, decided it was just the thing for getting to the Sistine Chapel on time and gave the drink his papal blessing. Coffee was on its way to worldwide popularity.

THE (UN)REAL THING

Coca-Cola was in trouble in the early 1980s. Its share of the cola market had slipped alarmingly. So, in 1985, a bright spark in the marketing department decided to reformulate Coke. The cola-drinking public went mental. The company got more than 400,000 complaints. So today they climbed down and agreed to bring back old Coke. However, all the brouhaha had alerted people to how much they liked Coke in the first place. By October, it was once again the number-one cola.

SAILING INTO HISTORY

Five ships full of colonists sailed from Leith today in 1698 in a bold bid to make Scotland a world power. The plan was to set up a lucrative trading post at Darien Bay in Panama. However, disease, foul weather and troubles with the natives – and other trading nations – led to disaster. Scotland ended up hugely in debt. But it was largely thanks to this debacle that the 1707 Act of Union came about, and the UK as we know it today came into being.

SIGN OF THE TIMES

13 Locals hated the advertising sign erected today in 1923 on Mount Lee in California. Its vulgar 45-foot-high letters could be seen for miles around. Thank goodness it was only temporary. However, 26 years later, it was still there and had become a bit of a landmark. So it was decided to renovate it – and drop off the last four letters (L-A-N-D) since the housing development it had promoted was long since sold. Now the 'HOLLYWOOD' sign is one of the world's most recognisable tourist icons.

BASTILLE BRAVADO

14 Storming the Bastille was actually a really, really bad idea. The hated Parisian fortress-prison was rather well defended and only had seven inmates in it today in 1789. Still, Paris was electric with rebellion and the ragtag crowd's ignorance led to unfounded, but ultimately triumphant, confidence. Soon the mob had surged into the outer courtyard, cut the chains of the drawbridge, beheaded the governor with a pocket-knife, and somehow this disastrous plan became the flashpoint of the French Revolution.

RUN OF A LIFETIME

15 It was the Olympic marathon in Stockholm today in 1912 and Japanese runner Shizo Kanakuri was thirsty. After stopping for a glass of water and a rest, he fell asleep, not waking until the race was over. Ashamed, he returned to Stockholm and sailed back to Japan. However, his failure to complete the course always nagged at his honour. So, in 1967, he returned and finished the race in a glorious new world record time of 54 years, 8 months, 6 days, 8 hours, 32 minutes and 20.3 seconds.

WHAT'S ALL THAT WATER DOING THERE?

16 Today in 1938, Douglas 'Wrong Way' Corrigan took off from Brooklyn headed for Long Beach, California. However, as his plane rose from the east runway, he neglected to turn round and simply kept going over the Atlantic. He landed near Dublin after a remarkable 28-hour flight. On the bright side, he'd fulfilled a long-standing ambition to cross the Atlantic that had been denied him by US aviation rules – but he always maintained he'd made a genuine mistake, and no one could prove otherwise …

WINDSOR NOT

17 During World War I, the British people somehow got the idea that King George V was pro-German. OK, the German Emperor Wilhelm II was his cousin, his family name was Saxe-Coburg-Gotha, and a German aircraft called the *Gotha G.IV* had just bombed London, so you could see their point. George decided to adopt a British name, and plumped for the name of one of his castles today in 1917 – Windsor is now accepted as the royallest of names.

TAKING THE MICKEY

18 The owner of the film company kept getting letters from fans who wanted to visit his studio. He had no idea why they wanted to do this but it seemed a shame to disappoint them. So he built a small play park with a boat ride and a couple of other attractions on an 8-acre plot over the road from the studio. It was, quite frankly, pathetic. So the studio owner thought a heck of a lot bigger and, today in 1955, Walt opened Disneyland.

BONNY WEE BEETLE

19 In the 1860s, French vineyards were under attack. By the time the disease had been identified as the *phylloxera* beetle today in 1868 by Jules Emile Planchon, as much as 90% of European vineyards had been destroyed. Wine and brandy became scarce and people were getting awfully thirsty. But this gap in the cellars was promptly plugged by canny Scotch distillers who upped whisky production to unprecedented levels. By the time the French industry recovered, whisky had widely replaced brandy as the spirit of choice.

PARK YOURSELVES ELSEWHERE

There's no upside to getting a parking ticket, right? Well, there is if you are Thomas Bryant of Corning, California. He managed to make it into a satisfying occasion on this day in 1980 by ordering the police department to quit its headquarters within 60 days. He owned the building.

MAKING A MONKEY OF THE LAW

It seemed like bad news today in 1925 for high school teacher John Scopes of Dayton, Tennessee. He was convicted of teaching evolution, which had recently been outlawed there. Reporters had flocked to the town to see big-name lawyers do battle to save a man's reputation. But in reality the trial was a publicity-raising stunt, for both local businesses and the anti-creationism cause. In this respect, the trial was a triumph for the guilty man – and Dayton businessmen.

JUST A GOOD OL' BOY

22 Today in 1921, a sheriff's deputy was killed in a raid on moonshiners in North Carolina. Bad news for him, and for David Williams, who was imprisoned for the crime. Williams used his sentence to pursue his passion for designing guns, encouraged by the warden (this was the USA!). He later helped create the M1 carbine, more than 6 million of which were produced, and their efficiency helped the USA achieve victory in the Pacific. Williams was pardoned after only eight years.

MADE IN PRISON

COOL THINKING

23 Two vendors at the sweltering 1904 St Louis World's Fair had a problem today. One, Ernest Hamwi, couldn't sell his hot Persian waffles to overheating visitors; while, at the next stall, Arnold Fornachau had a different problem – his ice cream was so popular he'd run out of plates to put it on. That's when Ernest had one of the coolest ideas in history – he rolled up one of his waffles and offered it to Arnold as an ice-cream holder, and so the ice cream cone was born.

MACHU MAN

24 Absolutely knackered after schlepping his way up a mist-covered Peruvian mountainside today in 1911, Hiram Bingham was beginning to regret his decision to go for a ramble with a local guide. So he was delighted when he discovered an ancient Inca city at the top. Unknown to anyone except the handful of natives living in the valley below, this turned out to be Machu Picchu, now one of the world's great heritage sites and a major tourist attraction.

HOW DOES IT FEEL TO BE ON YOUR OWN?

25 Bob Dylan must have thought he'd made a big mistake when he appeared on stage today in 1965 at the Newport Folk Festival with a rock band. As he launched into a new song, the audience of hardcore folkies booed in outrage that their hero had 'gone electric'. Dylan was so upset he didn't return to the Newport festival for 37 years. But 'Like a Rolling Stone' became not only his most popular song, but one of the most influential songs of all time.

HIGH-PRESSURE PHYSICS

26 Today in 1630, Italian physicist Giovanni Baliani discovered that he couldn't siphon water for more than 10 metres vertically. He wrote to the great Galileo about it, who set his student Evangelisa Torricelli to work trying to solve the problem. Eventually, after much experimenting, Torricelli realised that atmospheric pressure was the cause. His conclusion did not in any way allow the water to be siphoned any higher, so might be considered a failure. Apart from the fact that he had inadvertently invented the barometer.

HOME ON THE RANGE

27 It's the most militarised place on earth: 400 square miles stuffed with landmines, razor wire and watched by some seriously paranoid soldiers. The Korean Demilitarized Zone. But for the extremely rare Korean tiger, Amur leopard and Asiatic black bear, the DMZ is just dandy: there are no idiotic humans to shoot them or steal their food. In fact, since it was created today in 1953, the DMZ has become an Eden-like refuge for 2,900 plant species, 70 types of mammals and 320 kinds of birds.

BENEDICTUS'S BIG BREAK

28 Butterfingered French chemist Edouard Benedictus knocked a glass flask of cellulose nitrate off a high shelf today in 1903. However, instead of glass flying everywhere, the contents acted as an adhesive, holding the shattered pieces together. Benedictus found no takers for his new 'laminated glass', before World War I handily broke out today in 1914. His invention proved invaluable in gas masks, before taking the automotive industry by storm as the standard safety glass for windshields.

SUITS YOU, MADAM

29 Professional swimmer Annette Kellerman didn't see a problem when she strutted her stuff in a one-piece swimsuit on Revere Beach in Boston on this day in 1907. But the police thought differently and they arrested the Australian beauty for indecency. Not a great result for Kellerman on the face of it. But the papers went wild and she became a sensation, with her own swimwear line. Girls all over the world slipped them on and prudish Victorian swimwear laws were on their way out.

I AM THE RESURRECTION

30 Renowned thespian Patrick Mower was acting in the play *Deathtrap* today in 1987 when a faulty prop caused him severe embarrassment on stage. The play continued and his character was duly killed with a crossbow. Just before the final curtain, however, Mower resurrected his character and reappeared on stage to uncork a furious rant at the stage manager. This might have ruined the plot, but on the bright side it provided a drama-packed ending to what had been a pretty dull play.

THE BEST LAID PLANS ...

An Ayrshire farmer was having a miserable time trying to make ends meet on his poor-quality land. So he tried to become a surveyor but got dangerously ill. Next he helped in a shop until it burned down. Then, desperate to raise money for a passage to Jamaica, he self-published some poems today in 1786. The book was an instant success and Robert Burns became one of the world's most famous poets.

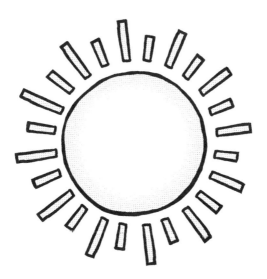

AUGUST

WE CAN'T REWIND, WE'VE GONE TOO FAR

1 'Video Killed the Radio Star' is a song by The Buggles, which laments the loss of the golden days of radio and predicts the demise of pop songs at the hands of technology. Ironically, however, the song's own longevity was forever secured today in 1981 when it became the star of a music and technology revolution – it was the first music video ever shown on MTV.

FRINGE BENEFITS

Eight fledgling theatre companies turned up in Edinburgh today in 1947, hoping to perform at the new arts festival. But since they weren't officially on the bill they were turned away. So they simply performed their plays anyway, on the 'fringe' of the real event. In the 60 years since, the Edinburgh Fringe has become the world's largest arts festival, with over 2,500 international shows from 60 nations in 258 venues.

JOINT WINNERS

Derek Redmond was dreaming of gold as he lined up for his 400 metres Olympic semi-final in Barcelona today in 1992. Sadly, he blew a hamstring on the back straight and could barely walk, let alone run. Yet he hobbled on in agony, determined to finish. Whereupon his dad jumped the barrier, shoving officials aside, and flung an arm round his son's shoulders. Father and son crossed the line together. The race was lost, but it was one of the most heart-warming sporting moments of all time.

LOVELY BUBBLY

Benedictine monk Dom Pierre Pérignon spent years trying to keep bubbles *out* of his wine – they were a sign of poor winemaking. But the Champagne region's cool climate meant the wine had to ferment for two years. Hence, the extra bubbles that, fortunately for us, he couldn't quite eliminate. The boozy Benedictine first uncorked his new brew today in 1693 and it was big hit at the French and English courts..

BERTHA IN THE DRIVING SEAT

It was 1888 and Karl Benz was having problems with his new 'Motorwagen' – its brakes barely worked and it couldn't climb steep hills. Worse, today his wife Bertha took the precious vehicle for a spin without asking. However, when she returned he found that she had stopped at a shoemaker's and asked him to nail leather onto the wooden brake blocks – thus inventing brake linings. She also suggested the car would climb better if Karl added another gear. With these improvements, the modern car was born.

A DEAD GOOD INVENTION

6 Thomas Edison was battling rival inventor George Westinghouse for control of the electrical power market. Edison favoured direct current, Westinghouse alternating current. When the first-ever execution by electric chair took place today in 1890, Edison craftily ensured it was done with his rival's technology to associate it with danger. But the event merely raised the profile of Westinghouse's invention, and it eventually won the 'War of the Currents' to become the standard technology.

LORD OF THE RINGS

Donald Currey was researching pines in Nevada's White Pine County, dating them by taking core samples. One tree, known as Prometheus, was proving tricky to core, so he asked forest rangers if he could cut it down. They said yes, and Currey felled it today in 1964. This was bad news for the tree, obviously, but it turned out to be great for science – the tree was at least 4,862 years old, making it the oldest individual organism ever discovered.

TOUCH TYPING

A three-year-old lad was playing with his father's tools when his hand slipped, plunging the point of an awl into his eye. The wound became infected and he soon lost his other eye too. But the bright lad was determined not to lose out on his education, and twelve years later he used a tool very much like that fateful awl to punch raised dots in paper to represent letters. Today in 1828, Louis Braille began teaching other blind children the reading system that bears his name.

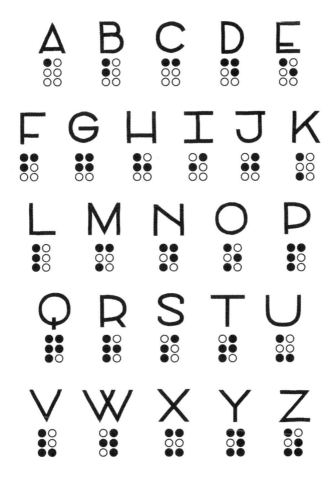

GALILEO GETS A PISA THE ACTION

9 It was a cowboy job from the start. Building on the Tower of Pisa started today in 1173 and within five years it was squint – the ten-foot foundations weren't nearly deep enough and the soil was unstable. After 200 years, the tower was nearly five feet off true. Still, if it hadn't been wonky, Galileo wouldn't have had such a perfect place to drop cannonballs from. He showed that differently sized objects fall at the same acceleration, disproving Aristotle's theory of gravity.

TUTU POOH-POOH BOO-BOO

10 Members of the San Francisco Ballet were gutted to read today in 1987 that their performance was absolutely slated by critic Heuwell Tircuit. He pulled no punches, calling the dancers 'dumpy' and 'potato-drenched' and the choreography 'dank'. Then a bright-eyed ballerina spotted that the performance that had so underwhelmed him was one that had been cancelled. Tircuit apparently made up his review instead of attending the performance. The fibbing critic was profoundly embarrassed – and got fired – but the ballet was dancing with joy.

THE BRILLIANT BOMBSHELL

11 Hedy Lamarr was a stunningly beautiful actress who appeared in the first ever nude cinema scene in the Czech film *Extase*. She then made a bad marriage to an Austrian arms dealer who kept her locked up and hosted Hitler at his mansion. But this awful treatment led her to flee to the US, where, today in 1942, she invented spread spectrum technology, used to stop the jamming of radio-controlled torpedoes and later in mobile phones and satellite encryption.

SEAFOOD DELIVERY SERVICE

12 Horrendous storms hit Annapolis in Maryland today in 1984, bringing high winds, torrential rain and violent waterspouts. George Messe was just one local resident who watched in fear from behind his curtains as a swirling waterspout roared in over his house from Chesapeake Bay. Once the spout had ruffled his roof tiles and passed over, he walked out to discover it had also deposited a rather delicious-looking lobster in his swimming pool.

READY, AIM ... FORK!

13 Harry Brearley was trying to make a better killing machine. It was 1913 and Britain was upping its arms production. Harry's job was to make a gun barrel that wouldn't wear out so quickly. And on this day he created a steel with 12.8 per cent chromium, highly resistant to heat and corrosion – perfect for killing people with. On the positive side, however, perfect for cutlery too. And soon stainless steel was in department stores as well as armouries across the land.

PIRATES UNPLUGGED

14 It was a sad day for the pirate DJs of Radio London today in 1967. Some very ungroovy new legislation pulled the plug on their maritime broadcasts for ever. However, those same DJs found jobs in mainstream radio, introducing pop to a whole generation of listeners. Tony Blackburn, Kenny Everett, John Peel, Ed 'Stewpot' Stewart, Dave Lee Travis and Tommy Vance all started off as pirates. Their antics also inspired the movie *The Boat That Rocked*, but we won't hold that against them.

PEACE, LOVE AND INDEBTEDNESS

15 John Roberts and Joel Rosenman were young men with a bit of cash who fancied being young men with a LOT of cash. So, together with a music promoter, they decided to organise a festival today in 1969. But the event spun out of control, with half a million people coming instead of the predicted 50,000, most of whom got in for free. In the end they lost $1.4 million on the event. However, to their eternal credit they could say that they had created Woodstock.

NON-MOP-TOP DROPPED

16 Pete Best was binned from The Beatles today in 1962. Bad news for him, of course, but great for Richard Starkey. Pete's hair was curly, and so, unlike the other three musicians, he couldn't wear it as a 'mop-top' – the hip look the boys wanted. So out he went, and in came the mop-toting Richard – or, as we know him, Ringo. The new-look band got almost instant attention and two months later they recorded their first single, 'Love Me Do'. The rest is music history.

ANYTHING VOUS CAN DO ...

17 Nicolas Fouquet was France's Minister of Finance and a bit of a show-off. He built a magnificent house on his estate, Vaux-le-Vicomte, with architecture and gardens on a staggering scale. It was so splendid that the jealous King Louis XIV promptly arrested Fouquet today in 1661 and threw him in prison. Terrible news for Fouquet, but terrific for lovers of baroque architecture – Louis insisted that Fouquet's designers build him an even more tremendous house. And so was born the magnificent palace of Versailles.

THIS PROMOTION SUCKS

18 Hoover launched a new promotion today in 1992: spend £100 and get two free flights. But the flights cost way more than the appliances and customers piled in, realising it was a cheap way to buy tickets. It was a PR and financial disaster for Hoover: they were pilloried for trying to renege on the promise, then lost £48 million on the scheme when they finally caved in. But for the 220,000 people who claimed their flights it goes down as the best promotion in history.

SAY 'FROMAGE'

19 Frenchman Louis Daguerre had perfected a nifty new way of recording fixed images, which he showed to the French government. They announced today in 1839 that the process would not be patented and was a gift 'free to the world'. This was very generous of them, if a little financially short-sighted. However, it did mean that large numbers of people were able to experiment with 'Daguerrotypes' without paying hefty royalty fees, and soon the new art of photography had exploded across the world.

PUBLICATION OF THE FITTEST

20 In 1858, Charles Darwin still hadn't written a book about his theory of natural selection, which he had first outlined 20 years before. Then he received an essay by Alfred Russel Wallace describing the same idea. The men published their first papers on the subject today, but Darwin was so horrified at almost being gazumped that he promptly pulled his finger out and quickly wrote *On the Origin of Species*, his revolutionary book on evolution which changed the scientific world for ever.

NO WONDER SHE'S SMILING

21 When da Vinci's *Mona Lisa* was stolen from the Louvre today in 1911, it was only a moderately famous painting. It was missing for two years until Louvre employee Vincenzo Peruggia was revealed as the thief when he tried to sell the painting to the Uffizi gallery. After being returned, the painting soon became extraordinarily popular and turned into a major draw for the Louvre. It is now the most famous and valuable painting in the world.

MONSTER PROFITS

22 St Columba was preaching God's word in the land of the Picts today in 565 when a huge monster came roaring at him out of the local lake. The good saint then used his faith to banish the beastie back into the water. Columba's fame ensured the story survived and people have been claiming to see monsters in Loch Ness ever since. Which has been a nice little earner for the local community, with 'Nessie hunters' bringing in millions in tourism every year.

THE CHARISMATIC CRIMINAL

23 When Jan Olsson and a comrade tried to rob a bank in central Stockholm today in 1973, it turned into a fiasco. The police were on the scene almost immediately and Olsson shot an officer before taking four hostages. Incredibly, as the crisis continued over the next five days, the hostages began to sympathise with their captors. Fortunately, they were released unharmed, and psychologists now had a new term to play with – 'Stockholm syndrome'.

CHEESED-OFF AND ONION

24 Chef George Crum was really annoyed at the Carey Moon Lake House in Saratoga Springs today in 1853. One very picky customer kept sending his plate of potatoes back, requesting that they be cut thinner and thinner. George finally saw red: he sliced the potatoes ultra thin, fried them until they were crispy and coated them in salt, determined to annoy the guest. To everyone's surprise, the customer asked for more. And so were born Saratoga chips – crisps to you and me.

THE TOXIC CURE

25 Being exposed to mustard gas in the World War I trenches must have been a horrific experience. However, medics did notice that soldiers exposed to mustard agents developed reduced numbers of white blood cells. Yale researchers spotted this again in the 1940s and reasoned that the agent might have a similar effect on cancer. Today in 1942, they gave patient 'J.D.', who had advanced lymphoma, an injection of a related compound, nitrogen mustard. His improvement was remarkable and chemotherapy was here to stay.

SILLY MONEY

 There was a shortage of rubber in World War II, so the hunt was on for a synthetic replacement. Engineer James Wright tried his best, but all he got was a gooey blob that bounced, stretched and picked up newsprint – useless. But a marketing consultant called Peter Hodgson later realised the goo would make a great toy. His 'Silly Putty' hit the headlines in the *New Yorker* today in 1950, shifted 250,000 in just three days and made him a millionaire.

THE RIGHT TYPE OF THINKING

27 When Christopher Sholes took some telegraph keys and piano wire and built the first typewriter, he created something that was ingenious, but also nearly useless. As soon as you tried to type at a half-decent speed, the lettered bars hit each other and jammed. This threatened to kill his new invention at birth. So Sholes decided to reconfigure the keyboard layout, splitting up the most commonly paired letters. The result was the QWERTY layout, which he patented today in 1878, and which remains the standard set-up.

FROZEN FILM FIND

28 Workers in Dawson City, Canada, were clearing out an old trash-filled swimming pool today in 1978 when they found hundreds of old movie reels. Obviously, the fragile 35mm nitrate films would be ruined after being dumped so unceremoniously ... But when experts looked closely they found many were in perfect nick precisely *because* they had been buried there, preserved by the Yukon's permafrost. Over 190 rare films from 1903–29 were saved, including the only surviving copy of an early Harold Lloyd film, *Bliss*.

RISING FROM THE ASHES

29 When the England cricket team lost for the first time at home to Australia today in 1882, it was a shock to national prestige. The *Sporting Times* published a mock obituary mourning the demise of 'English cricket, which died at the Oval'. It also joked that 'the body will be cremated and the ashes taken to Australia'. But without that defeat we may never have got to enjoy one of the most famous contests in world sport – the Ashes Test series.

YOUR IDEA BLOWS

30 Engine designer Hubert Booth was intrigued when he saw an American inventor demonstrate a new cleaning machine in a London theatre. This was meant to remove dust from carpets by blowing compressed air out, but was an utter disaster – all it did was blast the dust around and the front six rows burst out sneezing. Booth immediately realised the small adjustment needed – the device should suck, not blow – and, today in 1901, he patented the modern vacuum cleaner.

CRAZY CRUSADE

31 In 1212, according to legend, a Rhineland shepherd boy had a vision – an army of children would win back the Holy Land from the Muslims. Not the greatest of military strategies, but the idea caught the public imagination and thousands of children marched off to glory. It was a disaster – those that didn't die of hunger and cold were sold into slavery in Egypt on this day – but it did give rise to the classic story *The Pied Piper of Hamelin*.

SEPTEMBER

MUMMY SAID I MUST WEAR A HELMET

 Today in 2000 was a bad day for staff at the God's House Tower Archaeology Museum in Southampton who cycled to work: their bike rack was taken away. However, the 27-inch black rock with useful indentations that had propped up their cycles so neatly had just been identified by Egyptologists as a 2,700-year-old Egyptian statue of Kushite monarch King Taharqa. What Halfords were doing selling the thing in the first place has not been recorded.

A PLAGUE ON ALL YOUR HOUSES

2 The fire that started in London today in 1666 was certainly 'great' in its size – it destroyed the homes of 70,000 of the City's 80,000 inhabitants. But it was also pretty 'great' in that it only killed a handful of people while annihilating the city's rats. This was particularly good because the previous year an outbreak of plague, borne by rats' fleas, killed a sixth of London's population. No plague epidemics ever hit the capital after that. Apart from flower-sellers at traffic lights, obviously.

NOW WHERE DID I LEAVE THOSE DRUGS?

3 Next time someone nags you to tidy up, tell them you're actually saving the world. Slobbish scientist Alexander Fleming once went on holiday without bothering to clean up his lab. When he got back, today in 1928, all his Petri dishes had gone mouldy. But in one of them the rampant mould had killed the bacteria around it. Fleming had just discovered penicillin. Cures for syphilis, gangrene and tuberculosis were just around the corner and Fleming's untidiness would save millions of lives.

I'M JUST DROPPING IN

4 German Army Sergeant Helmut Schlecht was flying home on leave today in 1967 when he noticed his plane was passing right over his parents' house. Schlecht, an experienced parachutist, strapped on his chute, told the pilot to throttle back and jumped out. He was now facing serious trouble for this reckless act. Fortunately, as he was off duty at the time, all charges were dropped. And on the bright side, five minutes after bailing out he was enjoying a coffee in his parents' kitchen.

FOOTBALL TAKES A BIG STEP FORWARD

5 You may think American football looks dangerous today, but before 1906 it was so violent it was on the point of being banned. Mass collisions meant bruised heads and broken bones, and over 100 student players had died. The threat of a ban led to a major rule change, with the introduction of the forward pass on this day in 1906. The game became safer and more popular, creating the spectacle enjoyed by millions today.

THE CURTAIN FALLS ... FOR 18 YEARS

As soon as the prissy Puritans got the chance in the English Civil War, they closed the country's theatres today in 1642. So for 18 years the playhouses were empty – or, worse, torn down. However, when the restored monarchy reopened theatres in 1660, it ushered in a glorious age of English drama. Shakespeare and other Elizabethan classics were revived, Restoration comedy took off and, for the first time ever, women were accepted as actors.

WHO SAYS CRIME DOESN'T PAY?

Today in 1695 was no fun for the crew of the Mughal ship *Ganj-i-Sawai* – they were targeted by English pirate Henry Every. After a long chase and fierce battle, they were either murdered or captured and their ship plundered. This was clearly a bad thing. The only possible silver lining is that Every and his men escaped with so much loot – the biggest pirate haul in history – that they were all able to retire and never bothered anyone again.

IT'S LIFE JIM, BUT NOT AS WE KNOW IT

8 When the TV show *Star Trek* first appeared today in 1966, its host network NBC didn't really think much of the show and they cancelled it after just three seasons. But this was the best thing that could have happened to the show and its stars. Syndicated to continual reruns in order to make back some money, it gained a cult following and reached more people than it ever had originally. This new popularity led to the creation of the *Star Trek* film franchises.

DEBUGGING

9 The 5-ton Harvard Mark I was the first programmable digital computer in the US. Unfortunately, no sooner was this behemoth up and running than it broke down today in 1945. Fortunately, while the boffins scratched their heads, a programmer with common sense called Grace Hopper did a bit of poking and realised that there was a bug in the system – a dead moth was jamming a sprocket hole. She removed it and the computer ran perfectly for the next 15 years.

BAREFOOT BRILLIANCE

10 Marathon runner Abebe Bikila was only a last-minute addition to the Ethiopian team for the 1960 Rome Olympics. Sponsors Adidas had no running shoes that fitted him properly, so Bikila decided to run barefoot. And while this would have been a disaster for any other runner, it was actually the way that the country-born Bikila had trained for the race. He won in a record time of 2:15:16.2, becoming the first person from Sub-Saharan Africa to win an Olympic gold medal.

THE TASTE OF VICTORY

11 It was 1944, the French town of Dijon had just been liberated, and everyone fancied a celebration. But those rotten Germans had pinched all the red wine during the war. However, the new mayor – a war hero called Canon Felix Kir – took the less-than-palatable local white wine and added cassis (blackcurrant liqueur) to create a delicious new drink. Perhaps as a result, he remained mayor for 20 years. The drink eventually became known simply as 'Kir' and is still hugely popular today.

BATTLE OF THE BREAKFAST

12 In 1683, Vienna was besieged by 100,000 Ottoman Turks, and its terrified citizens were running low on supplies. The outlook was bleak. Then the attackers tunnelled under the walls – until some bakers raised the alarm, which helped save the city. When the Turks were later repelled on this day, the bakers celebrated by turning the crescent moon from their enemy's flag into a victory pastry – *et voila*! The croissant was born and was exported to France when Austrian Princess Marie Antoinette married Louis XVI.

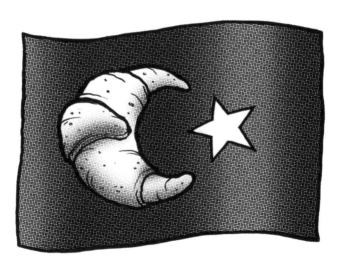

HE NEEDED THAT LIKE HE NEEDED A HOLE IN HIS HEAD

13 Bad day at work giving you a headache? Consider railroad foreman Phineas Gage, who, today in 1848, was packing dynamite into a hole with a three-feet-long, inch-thick tamping iron when the charge exploded. The bar shot up into his left cheek and out through the top of his head. Incredibly Gage survived. Alas, his personality changed – the formerly pleasant man became crude and abusive. But, years after his death, medical researchers used his skull to learn that different areas of the brain control different functions.

FLYING THE FLAG

14 Lawyer Francis Key looked on in despair today in 1814 as 19 British Navy ships pummelled the hell out of a US fort with rockets and mortar shells. The bombardment was violent and prolonged, but the US flag still stood at the end. The vivid experience inspired Key to write a patriotic poem, *Defence of Fort McHenry*. His stirring words were put to music and are now better known as *The Star Spangled Banner*, the American national anthem.

WRONG SORT OF LEGS ON THE TRACK

15 The Liverpool to Manchester Railway opened today in 1830, with dignitaries packing George Stephenson's *Rocket* and spectators lining the route. Alas, an unwary Liverpool MP called William Huskisson stumbled onto the track and got run over by the famous engine. Despite being 'rushed' for medical attention at the then incredible speed of 36 mph, poor Huskisson perished – the first victim of a rail accident – but the sensational story actually helped publicise train travel and gave a boost to this revolutionary mode of transport.

DOWN AND OUT, OUT AND UP

16 Immigrant life in 1911 New York was hard. Israel Baline was barely in his teens when his father died penniless. To up his takings from hawking newspapers, he began singing songs he picked up on the street. After a stint as a singing waiter, he finally got his big break as a songwriter, scoring his first big hit today in 1911 with 'Alexander's Ragtime Band'. A printer's error labelled him 'I. Berlin' and 'Irving' went on to become one of the greatest songwriters in American history.

IN A FIELD OF HIS OWN

17 Michael Biddell was nervous. He had entered his community fun run at the Waterlooville Festival today in 1994. Six marshals checked the mile-long course, a St John Ambulance crew got ready for emergencies and a VIP laid out the medals for the presentation ceremony. Luckily, it turned out that seven-year-old Michael was the only person who had bothered to enter. The gun went off, he took the lead and the delighted crowd roared the young champion home.

TIME FOR YOUR ANAL PROBE, MR PRESIDENT

18 Today in 1973, a peanut farmer called James Earl Carter filed an official report with the National Investigations Committee on Aerial Phenomena about some strange lights he'd seen in the sky. Four years later, Jimmy Carter became President of the United States. While some may be alarmed that the leader of the free world thought he'd seen little green men, on the upside it gives us *ET* fans a bit of hope that maybe there really is someone out there …

IS THIS A DISASTER I SEE BEFORE ME?

19 *Macbeth* isn't really known for its comedy value. Until today in 1980, that is. Peter O'Toole was the star of the Old Vic production that got what you would expect to be production-closing reviews: 'heroically ludicrous' was one of the kindest. However, it was so awful that the crowds came swarming, eager to see O'Toole's antics and the 'three sexy witches who … look as if they shop at Fortnum and Mason's'. The run sold out.

WE SHALL FIGHT THEM IN THE BATHTUBS …

20 As part of the British war effort to conserve fuel, the government asked people to bathe in no more than five inches of water from today in 1942. This made getting clean a lot harder. But it also led to lots of people sharing baths, which made getting dirtier much easier. Everyone soon 'mucked in' and even the royal family got in on the action, painting five-inch guide lines on all baths in the royal household.

MAKING A STAND

21 'A bit of a laugh' was the reason stand-up comedian Jacob Haugaard gave for standing in today's 1994 Danish general election. His manifesto included such plans as free beer, Renaissance furniture in IKEA and continuously green traffic lights. However, disaster beckoned when Jacob was actually elected and he had to somehow put his plans into practice. Happily, he was able to bring at least one of his madcap ideas onto the statute books: Nutella in all army field ration packs.

NEVER SAY DAI

22 Dai Brooks was enjoying a 2,000-foot parachute jump today in 1982 when the unthinkable happened – first his main chute then his reserve failed to open properly. Dai's descent was only slowed a little as he crashed to the ground. He survived, but was severely injured, spending the next three months in a plaster brace. On the bright side, though, he came out of hospital an inch *taller* than when he went in – thanks to the spinal therapy he received.

THE MONEY WANTED TO BE SPENT

23 Unemployed Joey Coyle of Philadelphia was delighted to find $1.2 million in used banknotes, which really had just fallen from the back of a lorry (well, a security van) today in 1983. When Joey was caught two weeks later, he had only $100,000 left. He was charged with theft. However, he was cleared: the jury accepted his claim of temporary insanity and even the judge was honest enough to say, 'I probably would have done the same thing in his position.'

SHE'S GOING TO BLOW HER TOP

24 Chemist Christian Schonbein's wife had banned him from doing any of his silly experiments in their kitchen. Ignoring his good lady, he was mucking about with some nitric acid today in 1845 when he spilled it. Terrified of getting caught, he hastily mopped it up with a cotton apron, which he hung over the stove to dry. The apron promptly disappeared in a blinding flash. He had just discovered nitrocellulose (he later called it guncotton), a vital ingredient in modern explosives and plastics.

A HOLE LOT OF HISTORY

25 A Bedouin shepherd was out on a hillside by the Dead Sea in 1946 when he carelessly fell into a hole. The hole turned out to be deep and the drop painful. But there was also a pot in the corner of the cavern containing some tatty-looking papers. These turned out to be the Dead Sea Scrolls: 972 original texts from the Hebrew bible. The Scrolls went online today in 2011, allowing everyone to view these amazing ancient manuscripts.

THE BOOB(S) THAT MADE
A BREAKTHROUGH

26 Today in 1816, a young lady came to Dr René Laennec and described some painful chest symptoms. So strict were the morals of the day that René could not bring himself to place his ear on her bosom, to listen to her heart in the normal fashion. But the resourceful medic quickly rolled up a piece of paper into a tube and used this instead. The heartbeat came through loud and clear, and René later fashioned a wooden version of this revolutionary new device – the stethoscope.

HOT STUFF

27 The American Civil War was a personal disaster for Edmund McIlhenny, a wealthy Southerner. The war ruined his business interests and he was forced to live with his in-laws on their Louisiana plantation, where the ex-financier was reduced to tending the garden. Ever enterprising, he decided to make a sauce from its best crop – a hot type of pepper. He sold the super-spicy sauce in tiny bottles and, today in 1870, patented his potion. Soon McIlhenny's famous Tabasco sauce was firing up taste buds worldwide.

BEWARE GREEKS BEARING LIGHTNING BOLTS

28 Today in 480 BC was truly a terrible day for the Persian navy, who with 1,000 ships to the Greeks' 370 were overwhelming favourites to win the Battle of Salamis. But thanks to some tactical brilliance by Greek commander Themistocles and a very fortunate storm, the Persians were routed. Greek culture flourished, bringing the brilliance of Plato and Aristotle, the beauties of Athens and the whole concept of democracy to the world at large.

A RATIONAL TRANSACTION

29 Before World War II, Britain imported 60 per cent of its food. With supplies being precious, today in 1939, every household in Britain had to register for rationing. Having a limited ration of food was obviously a bad thing for most people. But for the very poor it was a blessing, as they now had a guaranteed adequate supply of food. And by 1945 Britain was only importing 30 per cent of its food.

FIXED

30 Shotguns and sweating faces – that's how drugstore owner Henry Harmer knew the robbers meant business today in 1981. They were so strung out they wanted to take their fix right there in the store. So Henry hurried off to get their drugs – and some water to help wash the pills down. A few minutes later, the break-in turned into a sleepover. Henry had given one robber an almighty dose of tranquillisers and the other some sleeping pills and four ounces of rat poison.

OCTOBER

PERSIAN PUSSY

1 Today in 331 BC, Alexander the Great's army was getting pummelled by that of Persian Emperor Darius III – Greek civilisation was at stake. Although Darius was in a stronger position, when Alexander mounted a last desperate charge, for some reason he decided to abandon the battlefield. With him went his army's mojo and Alexander triumphed. Thanks to Darius's strange departure, the Persian threat pretty much evaporated and Greek culture with its arts and democratic ideas was free to make its mark on our world.

BET THAT LEFT A SOUR TASTE IN THE MOUTH

2 In the early 20th century, Italy produced 90 per cent of the world's citric acid from low-quality lemons. Then, today in 1916, a chemist called J.N. Currie pointed out that an ordinary fungus called *Apergillus niger* could produce citric acid when cultured. This was very bad news for thousands of Italian lemon growers (they went out of business), but good news for pharmaceutical, food and manufacturing companies – the price of citric acid fell by 75 per cent.

TOP MARKS FOR GOOD CONDUCT

3 Professor Hideki Shirakawa gave a student instructions for an experiment today in 1967 and told him to get on with it. The Tokyo student did, but accidentally added 1,000 times too much catalyst to the mix. Whoops – the experiment quickly went very, very wrong. But the silver film-like material that did appear was actually a new type of polymer that conducted electricity, now used in solar cells and mobile phones, and its discovery netted the professor a Nobel Prize ... which seems a bit unfair on the student.

GO SCULPT IT ON THE MOUNTAIN

Gutzon Borglum was a sculptor with big ideas – mountain-sized. He was commissioned for a 90x190-foot bas-relief of confederate general Robert E. Lee on a hillside in Georgia and work started well. However, he fell out with his patrons – the Ku Klux Klan – and departed, his work being erased by his replacement. But Borglum had learned the skills he needed to sculpt on a massive scale. So, today in 1927, he started a new, even bigger project that would be a real landmark in his career – Mount Rushmore.

A DIFFERENT TYPE OF DAY OFF

Hard lines for anyone who had a nice holiday booked for today in 1582. When they went to bed last night it was the 4th, but they would have woken up this morning on the 15th. The Julian calendar established by Caesar wasn't accurate enough and had gained 3 days every 400 years, so the spring equinox was moving steadily towards the middle of winter. The new Gregorian calendar that replaced it is accurate to one day every 3,300 years.

CHATEAU ATOMIQUE

6 With Cold War paranoia at a peak, today in 1961, President John F. Kennedy advised American families to build bomb shelters to protect them from atomic fallout in the event of a nuclear war. Many house builders tried to cash in on the crisis by offering a bomb shelter with new homes. Scary times. Happily, most of these suburban bunkers were later decommissioned, but many householders were pleased to discover that the cool, subterranean structures make absolutely perfect wine cellars.

THE TREASURE IN THE ATTIC

7 A US librarian inherited six huge trunks from her grandfather. She decided to inspect all the contents in honour of the old man, but the job was so boring it took her more than three decades to get through them. What a slog. It all became worth it in 1990 when she discovered a 665-page bundle that turned out to be the first half of Mark Twain's original handwritten manuscript of *Huckleberry Finn*. The pages were soon reunited with the second half of the book in a Buffalo library.

HOT CHOCOLATE

8 Engineer Percy Spencer was working on radar technology when he turned on his radiation-producing magnetron and something scary happened – the chocolate bar in his pocket instantly melted. Rather than switch it off in a panic, Spencer simply fired it up again and proceeded to have a jolly time exploding eggs and popping corn. Eventually, he put a box around the magnetron and marketed it as a new way to cook food – the microwave. He patented it today in 1945.

BACK TO ... OH, BUGGER IT

9 Today in 1993 became the first day of Prime Minister John Major's new moral initiative – 'Back to Basics'. This crusade aimed to encourage law and order, community spirit and high ethical standards, particularly from those in the public eye. It crashed and burned within a couple of years as more than a dozen top Tories were exposed in some sort of juicy scandal, including David Mellor, Neil Hamilton and Jonathan Aitken. It gave the rest of us a jolly good laugh, though.

SORRY, LOVE, GOD TOLD ME TO DO IT

10 How can leaving out one little word cause so much trouble? Robert Barker and Martin Lucas were fined £300 and lost their printers' licence today in 1633, just for leaving the word 'not' out of the Bible. Admittedly, it did leave the Seventh Commandment reading: 'Thou *shalt* commit adultery', but anyone can make a mistake. It's not known whether any straying husband ever quoted it in his defence, but it certainly would have brought a smile to the face of many a bored churchgoer.

YOU SAW THEM HERE FIRST

11 US TV network NBC had a major problem on its hands when their big star Johnny Carson cancelled his weekend shows so he could take more time off. Needing something to fill the gap, they took a chance on a chaotic live comedy show, which first appeared tonight in 1975. It was an instant smash, and *Saturday Night Live* went on to launch the careers of many famous names, including Dan Aykroyd, Eddie Murphy, Bill Murray and Mike Myers.

THE LOST CONTINENT

12 Today in 1492, a triumphant Christopher Columbus landed in India and established a vital trading colony for the Spanish crown … er, actually, no. Columbus was 5,000 miles off course and had, in fact, discovered San Salvador in the Caribbean. Still, if he'd known how far it really was from Spain to India, he would probably never have set off. It seems that ignorance really is bliss, at least when it comes to discovering the Bahamas.

INSPIRATION ON VACATION

13 Today in 1665, Cambridge University had to be closed because an outbreak of bubonic plague was despatching undergrads left, right and centre. Nasty – but it did force Isaac Newton to return home to Lincolnshire where he used his free holiday to have one of the most inspired brainstorms in scientific history. He made prodigious advances in optics, physics and astronomy, laying the foundations for his famous *Principia Mathematica* – and inventing calculus for good measure.

HAROLD'S HURRY

14 Saxon England was in big trouble today in 1066. As soon as King Harold had repelled Vikings in the north, he had to return south to deal with William of Normandy at Hastings. His army was knackered, they lost the battle and Harold was killed. Bad news for the Saxons – their entire culture was usurped. But great long-term news for the country, as the Normans built magnificent castles and cathedrals, transformed the language and helped raise England from a north European backwater to a world power.

THE IDEA THAT STUCK

15 Coming back from a country walk with half the forest stuck to you is a bit of a pain. But when Swiss engineer George de Mestral arrived home covered in prickly burrs in 1941, he was fascinated by how the strands of the burrs caught onto cloth. Eight years of experimenting later, de Mestral finally produced two strips of fabric, one with hooks and the other containing loops. When the two strips were pressed together, they stuck. He filed his patent for Velcro today in 1952.

YOU'RE A SAUCY ONE

 Back in 1838, two chemists concocted a curry powder recipe. The result was disgusting. They tried diluting the potion into a sauce, but there was no improvement. The barrel was exiled to the basement. A few years later, the chemists stumbled over it and decided to try the sauce again; it had fermented, mellowed and was now positively delicious. They were John Lea and William Perrins, and their Worcestershire sauce has been produced in the same factory since this day in 1897.

OIL IN A GOOD CAUSE

When OPEC oil ministers agreed an oil embargo and a huge cut in production today in 1973, it took only a few months before the price of oil quadrupled and there was an energy crisis. But it did lead to greater interest in renewable energy and spurred on research in solar power and wind power. Japan shifted from oil-intensive industries to invest in electronics. US drivers demanded lighter and more fuel-efficient models and by 1980 huge gas-guzzling cars were outnumbered by compact hatchbacks.

SHOW ME THE MONEY

18 A South African woman living in LA was in a bank when the teller refused to cash her cheque. The woman was outraged, and proceeded to make quite a scene. The teller still refused to pay out. Things weren't all bad, though. A talent scout handed her his card as she stormed out and soon Charlize Theron had her first major movie role in *2 Days in the Valley*, which was released today in 1996. Bet she probably banks elsewhere now.

THIS IDEA IS DYNAMITE

19 Studying explosives isn't for the nervous. Young Swedish chemist Alfred Nobel was exploring the possibilities of nitroglycerin when a massive explosion at the family factory in 1864 killed five people, including his younger brother Emil. The tragedy focused Alfred on finding a safe way to manufacture and use the volatile compound. He soon discovered that a rock mixture called *kieselguhr* (diatomaceous earth) absorbed and stabilised the liquid. He patented this as dynamite today in 1867. It would revolutionise the construction and mining industries.

LONG TIME IN THE TELLING

When *The Hobbit* sold millions, J.R.R. Tolkien's publishers asked him to bash out a 'new Hobbit'. He agreed, but did warn them that he wrote slowly and that this one might take him a while longer. 'No problem,' they replied. He started straight away, in 1937, but it wasn't until today in 1955 that the final volume of *The Lord Of The Rings* was published. It was worth the 18-year wait. It shifted more than 150 million copies, making it the third best-selling novel of all time.

STRAIT TALKING MAN

Adventurer Ferdinand Magellan was furious after being booted out of court in his native Portugal. So, when neighbouring Spain were looking for a bold sea captain, he jumped at the chance to stick one over on his old patron. Today in 1520, he and his crew discovered the strait that now bears his name. Although Magellan died during the voyage, one of his ships rounded the Cape of Good Hope to complete the first ever circumnavigation of the globe.

THE CHIPS ARE DOWN

22 'My homework blew up' is a lame excuse. However, for PhD student Jamie Link at the University of California, it was not only true, it was also the best thing about it. One of the silicon chips she was working on accidentally shattered into tiny pieces. But the 'smart dust' that resulted can monitor the purity of drinking water, detect hazardous chemical agents in the air, and locate and destroy tumour cells in the body. Her discovery won top prize at the Collegiate Inventors Competition today in 2003.

STICKING TO HIS GUNS

23 Dr Harry Coover was trying to find a plastic to make precision gun sights. He got frustrated because the material he was working with, called cyanoacrylate, was just too sodding sticky. It wasn't until he was later working in a Kodak chemical plant that he realised that being insanely sticky could actually be a *good* thing. The glue was patented today in 1956 and released as 'Eastman 910'. Someone then pointed out such a terrible name would never stick – so it was redubbed 'Superglue'.

PEACE PLEASE

24 The international organisation The League of Nations completely failed to prevent World War II, but if there was one lesson to be learned from those six tragic years it was that some sort of body promoting peace and cooperation was necessary. So, today in 1945, the charter was ratified of a new organisation aimed at saving mankind from itself – the United Nations. The UN's blue-helmeted peacekeepers have since saved thousands of lives in conflicts around the world.

WHICH VALLEY OF DEATH, SIR?

A cock-up over exactly which guns Lord Cardigan was meant to be attacking led to the ill-fated Charge of the Light Brigade today in 1854. Cardigan and 672 riders galloped into a narrow valley surrounded on three sides by 5,240 Russian cavalry. Carnage ensued. After regrouping, only 195 men were still with horses. It was a military disaster, but the event fired the public imagination, coming to typify a very British sort of bravery. It also inspired Tennyson's famous poem.

KING OF THE CAKES

On the run from Viking invaders in the 870s, King Alfred took shelter with a peasant woman. She left him to watch some cakes, and the preoccupied king let them burn. Unaware of his identity, the crone gave him a bollocking. This shook him from his torpor and shocked him into action: he went out and gave the Vikings what for, reunited the kingdom and was proclaimed 'The Great'. Today was set aside as a feast day in his honour.

ROYAL ROTTER

27 Today in 1936, American socialite Wallis Simpson filed for divorce from her second husband so she could marry Edward VIII, causing a scandal and constitutional upset. But, in reality, Britain dodged a bullet when Edward abdicated. The first thing he did after marrying Simpson was go to Germany and meet Hitler. He reviewed SS troops and gave full Nazi salutes. Hitler later said, 'His abdication was a severe loss for us.' He was eventually dispatched to the Bahamas, which he called 'third class'.

JUDE THE OBSCURE

28 Judas Thaddeus was a loyal apostle of Christ and was later canonised as St Jude. Unfortunately, people tended to mix him up with Judas Iscariot, the disciple who betrayed Jesus. So, for centuries, hardly anyone prayed to old St Jude. Happily, this was sorted when the Church realised he'd be perfect as the patron saint of lost causes.

STOCK PRICES ARE FALLING

29 It was the dedication of the Statue of Liberty today in 1886 and New York was having a celebratory parade. But the hard-working brokers in financial firms were far too busy to buy any confetti or flowers, so they simply lobbed the scrap paper from their ticker-tape machines out of the windows of their Manhattan office blocks. This spontaneous outbreak of littering actually looked really cool, and so the tradition of the ticker-tape parade was established.

WELLES'S WONDERFUL WAR

30 When 23-year-old Orson Welles broadcast his radio version of *The War of The Worlds* today in 1938 it caused panic. The story of an alien invasion of earth was presented as a live newscast of actual events and thousands of people were genuinely frightened, believing it to be real. For Welles, though, the chaos was a godsend. He rocketed from radio actor to Hollywood hotshot and was soon able to launch his film career with *Citizen Kane*, widely acclaimed as one of the greatest movies ever made.

THEY'RE BREEDING LIKE RABBITS

 When Englishman Thomas Austin moved to Australia, he found he couldn't hunt rabbits – the creatures were unknown in the country. What rotten luck. So, today in 1859, he introduced just 12 bunnies for sport. The bunnies did what bunnies do best and soon there were so many in Victoria that 2 million could be killed without halting the growth of the species. They devastated native crops and altered the ecosystem of an entire continent. On the positive side, at least Australia's schoolchildren had lots of flop-eared new friends.

NOVEMBER

SPLASH THE CASH

1 In 1947, Jackson Pollock was a 36-year-old artist whose shows were known for only one thing – poor reviews. One day he became so frustrated with a poor picture that he grabbed a pot of household gloss paint and poured it all over the canvas. Bingo. Pollock had just discovered 'drip' painting, and art fans went wild for it. Today in 2006, his work *No. 5, 1948* sold for $140 million, the highest amount ever paid for a painting.

TRIAL BY TITILLATION

2 When Penguin Books published the unexpurgated edition of D.H. Lawrence's *Lady Chatterley's Lover* in 1960, they were prosecuted under the Obscene Publications Act – a potential disaster for them. The subsequent trial was a sensation, but the jury were as keen to read it as everyone else and took about 20 seconds to return a 'not guilty' verdict today. This was terrific news for fans of high-brow hanky-panky, freedom of speech activists and for Penguin themselves. They sold out their entire stock of 200,000 copies in hours.

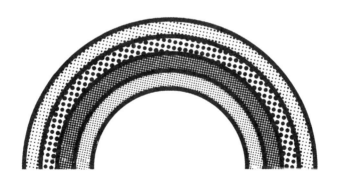

FLOATING IN A TIN CAN

Today in 1957 was a bad one for Laika, a mongrel dog. Sealed in a glorified tin can and fired into the sky, her oxygen was running out and it was getting very hot: unsurprisingly, she died. On the bright side, perhaps, as Laika's doggy soul left her mortal frame, she might have been happy to have played a part in a stratospheric technological leap forward. Laika had just become the first creature to venture into space, aboard Sputnik 2. Then again, she might not.

THE TILL BUILT TO KEEP FINGERS OUT

Business was bad for saloon owner James Ritty of Dayton, Ohio. This was principally because his bar staff were pinching a large proportion of his takings. Most managers would simply have fired the workers, but Ritty used this setback more creatively. He invented the cash register, which he patented today in 1879. His company later became the National Cash Register Company, NCR, which is still going strong today – mostly they make 'hole-in-the-wall' machines, which *give* you money …

WHAT A NICE GUY

5 There was no real personal upside for Guido 'Guy' Fawkes when he was caught red-handed today in 1605 with 36 barrels of gunpowder beneath the House of Lords. Tortured before suffering the grisly fate of hanging, drawing and quartering, his final days and hours would have been unimaginably painful. The good news for James I was that he wasn't blown up. The great news for us is that we got a nice excuse to have a jolly good fireworks party and bonfire.

YOU HAVE WON SECOND PRIZE IN A BEAUTY CONTEST

6 Elizabeth Magie hated the way property was bought and sold in America in the early 20th century, considering it to be 'land-grabbing'. So she created a board game to educate people, particularly children, about the unfairness of the market. It was called *The Landlord's Game* and she sold it for $500 today in 1935. Which was not bad, but it was even better for Charles Darrow, who pretty much copied her ideas, turned them into his own version called *Monopoly* and became a millionaire.

TROUBLED BRIDGE OVER WATER

The Tacoma Narrows bridge was the third-longest suspension bridge in the world, but no sooner was it built than it began to wobble. Then, today in 1940, in a wind of just 40 mph, the whole thing began to whip and twist before spectacularly collapsing. But its demise taught engineers a lot about bridge aerodynamics, which has improved the designs of all structures since. Plus, the highway deck that plunged into Puget Sound has formed an environmentally valuable artificial reef.

X MARKS THE SPOT

Next time your plane lands safely having not been blown out of the air by terrorists, remember messy old Wilhelm Roentgen. The physicist was experimenting with cathode rays in his cluttered workspace today in 1895 when he noticed something glowing on the other side of his lab. It was a small cardboard screen painted with barium platinocyanide, left over from another experiment he hadn't bothered tidying away. Two weeks later, he took the world's first X-ray picture, of his wife Anna's hand.

BADLY BRIEFED

9

In 1989, East Germany's government saw the democratic writing on the Berlin Wall. As a concession they decided to allow East Berliners visas only for *visiting* West Germany. The propaganda minister announced this at a press conference today, but the note he was given to read out was ambiguous, suggesting that all East Germans could now *freely* travel abroad. The broadcast was barely over when tens of thousands of people swamped the ill-prepared guards at the checkpoints and the Wall was history.

ODE TO MY HOPELESSNESS

10

George Wither was a spectacularly bad poet. However, his lack of talent once saved his life. Fighting on the Parliamentary side in the English Civil War, he was captured by Royalists today in 1642 and sentenced to death. Then the Royalist poet Sir John Denham begged the King to spare Wither's life. 'Why?' asked His Majesty. 'Because whilst George Wither lives, I shall not be the worst poet in England.' The King agreed and Wither went free.

CAMEL CALAMITY

11 In 1857, Lieutenant Edward Beale was ordered to try out camels as military pack animals in the US desert. At the same time, he had to build a 1,000-mile wagon road to help settlers move west. The camel idea was a failure – they scared the army horses and were generally too grumpy to be useful. However, Beale did manage to get the wagon trail built, and it later became a major part of US Route 66, the famous long-distance road that was established today in 1926.

A WHALE OF A PROBLEM

12 When a dead sperm whale washed up in Oregon today in 1970, the local Highway Division turned up to dispose of the carcass. Fortunately for connoisseurs of funny videos, they decided to blow it into seagull fodder with half a ton of dynamite. They failed in a spectacularly entertaining fashion – chunks of blubber rained down on spectators and one piece flattened a Cadillac a quarter of a mile away. The clip has been viewed online more than 350 million times.

SHOCK CURE

John 'Mad Jack' Mytton was the 19th-century eccentric who made other eccentrics seem like accountants. He often went hunting naked, drank eight bottles of port a day and once rode a bear to a dinner party. Suffering a severe attack of hiccups today in 1832, he decided to cure it by setting his own nightshirt on fire. He suffered nasty burns before his servant beat the flames out. Although in dreadful agony, he was at pains to point out: 'Well, the hiccup is gone, by God.'

ANNE EXCELLENT IDEA

Poor Catherine of Aragon had produced six children for Henry VIII but only one girl, Mary, had lived beyond infanthood. Desperate for a male heir, Henry asked Pope Clement VII for an annulment of his marriage. Clement refused. So Henry promptly defied the Pope and married Anne Boleyn anyway today in 1832. This break with Rome was bad news for English Catholics, of course, but good for England's sovereignty and Protestantism – it was the move that ultimately led to the creation of the Church of England.

THE QUIET REVOLUTION

15 A car accident put Brian Eno in hospital, bedridden and in a cast. He was given an album of harp music and, summoning all his strength, he put the record on the turntable and returned to bed – only to discover it was almost inaudible and he was now too exhausted to turn it up. But the quiet music worked its magic and led Eno to create his landmark album *Discreet Music* (released today in 1975), pretty much inventing ambient music in the process.

WRITER'S REPRIEVE

16 A young Russian writer was arrested in 1849 and charged with conspiracy against the government. Sentenced to death by firing squad today, he was led to the execution ground and roped to a post. The command to load was given. 'Aim!' ... A long pause. Suddenly, a horseman approached with a message – the death sentence was commuted to penal servitude. The horrendous experience gave Fyodor Dostoyevsky a profound love of life. He went on to write several classic works of literature, including *Crime and Punishment*.

FIGHTING THE GOOD FIGHT

17 Sweden declared war on Britain today in 1810, not very sporting considering the two nations were old allies. Sweden were basically bullied into it by France, but they had no desire to paralyse their own economy by attacking their biggest trading partner, so, while they *declared* war, they never got round to doing any of the fighting bit. So no battles, or even skirmishes, and the whole thing was brushed under the carpet soon after. The Anglo-Swedish War goes down as the most civilised in history.

SMUGGLER'S LUCK

18 Harry Paulet was smuggling goods across the Channel today in 1759 when he spotted a French warship sneaking away from a British blockade at Brest. Paulet later passed the British ship *Royal George* and, as a patriot, he decided to sacrifice his profits and risk arrest. He went on board and told Admiral Hawke what he had seen. His information helped Hawke rout the French and Paulet, as a reward, was sent on his way with his illicit cargo intact.

EDSEL NO SELL

19 The Ford Edsel was the wrong size, the wrong price, the wrong style and it was promoted badly – as cars go, it was a non-starter. So, despite pumping $400 million into its development and production, Ford just couldn't sell the cars. Today in 1959, the entire line was discontinued. The scale of the disaster, however, ensured that the Edsel would live on – it was such a catastrophe that it is now used in business classes as a vivid example of how *not* to market a product.

A WHALE OF A PROBLEM

20 Being a Nantucket whaler in 1820 was a hard life. And for the crew of the *Essex* it was about to get much harder today. An 80-ton sperm whale turned on the ship, rammed it and sank it. The 20-man crew took to small boats and were forced into murder and cannibalism to survive, with only eight of them making it back. The only upside is that their tale was immortalised in one of the great works of literature, Herman Melville's *Moby Dick*.

HOLEY MACKEREL

21 Fishing in the 10-foot-deep freshwater Lake Peigneur was good, but limited. Then, today in 1980, an oil rig drilled through the bottom of the lake and into a huge mine. The entire lake drained into this hole, taking 65 acres of land with it. Then water from the local bay came flooding in, filling the lake with salty ocean water. Within two days the lake was 1,300 feet deep, salty and home to many species of fish that hadn't been there previously.

THE GEEK STRIKES BACK

22 'Forget traditional animation, we need to make the movie with computers!' said John Lasseter to his bosses at Walt Disney Studios in the early 1990s. His bosses fired him on the spot. The good thing is that Lasseter ended up working for Steve Jobs, someone who really believed in computers. He wrote and directed *Toy Story* with Pixar (released today in 1995), the first fully computer-generated feature, which earned $350 million and an Oscar. In 2006, Lasseter became the chief executive of Walt Disney Studios.

WHAT'S IN A NAME?

23 'You'll go down like a lead balloon.' So said Keith Moon about the prospects of Jimmy Page's new supergroup. 'You're right!' thought Jimmy, and promptly changed the group's name from the 'New Yardbirds' to 'Led Zeppelin'. Embracing Keith's doom-laden judgement was a rocking good move – today in 1968, Led Zeppelin secured a $200,000 advance from Atlantic Records, the biggest deal of its kind for a new band, and over the next 12 years they would become one of the biggest-selling rock acts in history.

HOME ON THE RANGE

24 The US Army's M247 'Sergeant York' mobile anti-aircraft gun was one of the worst weapons ever built. Its radar couldn't distinguish trees from helicopters and, at a demonstration today in 1984, it aimed its barrel at the VIPs in the stand. It couldn't even hit a target hovering directly overhead. After a fortune had been wasted, the project was finally cancelled, but there was a bright side. The air force found the 50 prototype vehicles made excellent targets on their bombing ranges.

SLINKY THINKING

25 Richard James, a US Navy engineer in World War II, was trying to stop delicate instruments being thrown about his ship in rough seas. Nothing worked. Then he knocked a big spring over and it flip-flopped from his bench onto a shelf, then some books, to stand neatly on the floor – a lightbulb moment. After the war, he borrowed $500 to produce more of the springs. He demonstrated it for the first time today in 1945, and 400 Slinky toys sold within 90 minutes.

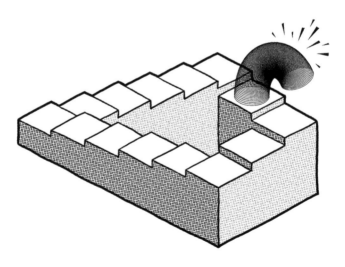

WHERE DO THESE STEPS GO?

26 By 1922, Howard Carter had been digging in Egypt's Valley of The Kings for five years without finding anything significant. His patron, Lord Carnarvon, was fast losing patience and it looked like this season would be their last. Then a workman was clearing up in preparation for their departure when he noticed a step descending into the desert. Carter investigated and today he and Lord Carnarvon became the first people to enter the tomb of Tutankhamun in over 3,000 years.

UP FROM THE DEPTHS

27 With German forces humbled at the end of World War I, Britain interned the 74 ships of their High Seas Fleet in Scapa Flow, Orkney, today in 1918, while they worked out how best to use them. Unfortunately, the Germans had other ideas and scuttled the entire fleet a few months later. Britain was furious – it was hugely expensive to salvage the ships and most were scrapped. However, seven vessels remained on the sea floor and these rotting wrecks now constitute one of the world's best dive sites.

FROM SMUT TO STARDOM

28 In 1907, the Gem Theater in Massachusetts was a dilapidated dump with an unsavoury reputation for hosting racy burlesque shows. It was despised in the community, and because the locals hated the place so much Lazar Meir was able to buy it cheaply. He reopened it as a movie theatre today, it was a success, and Meir soon owned a chain of cinemas. As Louis B. Mayer, he then founded a film studio, MGM, which would create some of the greatest movie legends of all time.

HUNGRY FOR CHANGE

29 The TV report by Michael Buerk was heartbreaking: hundreds of thousands of people in Ethiopia were dying of starvation. But, in a positive response to the tragedy, Bob Geldof and Midge Ure knocked out a tune, got their pals to sing on it and released it today in 1984. 'Do They Know It's Christmas?' by Band Aid became the biggest-selling single in history, raising millions for Africa and launching a new generation of fundraising songs and concerts.

FRESH THINKING

30 When Earl Tupper created a range of sealable plastic bowls (patented today in 1954), he thought he was on to a winner. But most major retailers turned their noses up at him. Frustrated by this failure, he pulled his goods from the few shops that did stock them and tried a different tactic. Soon 'Tupperware Parties', where the hostess got commission for all goods sold to her friends, were all the rage. Plastic food boxes made it into the mainstream and husbands made it to the pub.

DECEMBER

BUGGER OFF, BOYCOTT

1 In 1880, English landlords were setting extortionate rents for their Irish tenant farmers. The farmers banded together into the Land League. One early target was a particularly brutal estate manager in County Mayo. The Land League convinced all local residents to refuse to sell him goods, work in his fields or indeed speak to the man. The manager's will broke and he bolted for home on this day. His name was Charles Boycott and an effective new campaigning tactic had just been born.

SHE FELT A BIT DOWN

2 Poor Elvita Adams was so depressed today in 1979 that she leaped to her death from the 86th floor of the Empire State Building – well, she tried. No sooner had she stepped from the 1,472-foot skyscraper than a freak gust of wind buffeted her back onto a 30-inch ledge on the 85th floor. This unexpected turn of events seems to have turned Elvita's situation around – she took it as a sign from God and went on to lead a happier life.

MINERS' MAJOR MANOEUVRE

3 In 1854, gold miners at Ballarat, Australia, began protesting against the hefty cost of licence fees and their lack of representation. This led to violence at the Eureka Stockade today, when a government regiment routed the rebels, killing 22 of them. But, at the ringleaders' trial, thousands of supporters demonstrated on their behalf. They were found not guilty – the tide had truly turned. Within a year, all but one of their demands were met and the event was a huge stepping-stone towards democracy in Australia.

DEEP WATER DREAMING

Deep Purple were in Switzerland in 1971 to record in a mobile studio at the Montreux Casino. But a lunatic fan with a flare gun set fire to the casino's ceiling during a Frank Zappa concert and the whole place burned down. A few days later, bassist Roger Glover had a dream in which smoke from the fire spread across Lake Geneva. This inspired the song 'Smoke on the Water', a major hit for the band containing one of the most famous riffs of all time.

GREATNESS THRUST UPON THEM

John Heminge and Henry Condell were two unemployed actors with a cash-flow problem. So they decided to publish the plays of an old friend who had recently died. He'd been popular, but no one at the time thought he was particularly amazing. They found missing scripts and spent months compiling the most accurate versions of texts. Happily for them, the book they published today in 1623 was a success. And happily for us, it brought together the works of William Shakespeare for the first time.

LOVE IS THE DRUG

6 Barbara was in an embarrassing situation; a young German chemist called Adolf von Baeyer had made a weird request of the Munich waitress. No, not that sort of request! He was conducting experiments with urea – found in pee. Barbara overcame her misgivings to augment his supplies and Adolf never forgot her generosity. Indeed, he named the big discovery he made today in 1864 after her – barbituric acid. This would later become a key ingredient in many plastics and, of course, barbiturates.

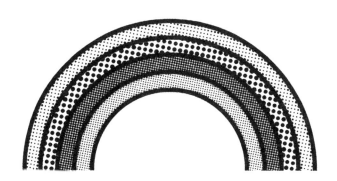

PLASTIC FANTASTIC

7 Shellac is a resin that was very useful as a colorant, glaze and electrical insulator. It was also very pricey. Chemist Leo Baekeland tried synthesising shellac, but his experiments just yielded a useless doughy material that set hard after being heated. At first Baekeland was distraught. Then he realised that his 'Bakelite', which he patented today in 1909, might have thousands of uses, from telephones to phonograph records. He was right, and Bakelite marks the beginning of the modern plastics industry.

HOOP DREAMS

8 The New England winter of 1891 was a particularly harsh one. Dr James Naismith was failing to keep his rowdy gym class occupied on yet another sleet-sodden day. He decided he needed a new game, one which could be played indoors and which would be athletic without having the violence of full contact. He got a soccer ball and two peach baskets, which he fixed to a 10-foot-high railing in the gym. And so, from the depths of a dark winter's day, basketball was born.

SALES ARE OUT OF THIS WORLD

9 Remember the moment in *ET* (released today in 1982) when Elliott lures the alien into his house with a trail of little sweets? Director Steven Spielberg initially asked Mars for permission to use M&Ms in that scene but, incredibly, they turned him down. So Mars missed the marketing opportunity of a lifetime as instead Spielberg used the recently launched and comparatively little-known candy called Reese's Pieces. After the film was released, sales of the upstart rival rocketed by more than 65 per cent.

LIFE'S A GAS

Sam Cooley attended a stage show today in 1844 in Hartford, Connecticut, and volunteered to inhale nitrous oxide – 'laughing gas'. He then larked about for the amusement of the audience, but also gashed his leg nastily on a chair. On the plus side, in the audience was dentist Horace Wells, who realised the gas had prevented Cooley feeling any pain. He later used the compound as an anaesthetic while he removed his own tooth. The use of anaesthesia during surgery soon took off.

THE VOYAGE THAT RAN DRY

It's difficult to see a positive side to running out of beer. But consider the ship full of would-be American colonists having a terrible time in the North Atlantic today in 1620. They were searching for the best place for their colony but were running low on supplies. Particularly ale. The sight of their empty beer barrels convinced them to head straight for the nearest bit of coast. Which is how the Pilgrims on the *Mayflower* established their famous colony at Plymouth Rock, Massachusetts on this day.

FOR SO IT IS WRITTEN

In 1917, a British force aiming for Jerusalem was bogged down at a heavily defended place called Michmash. Major Vivian Gilbert turned in despair to his Bible. There he read how Saul had also encountered 'the Philistines encamped in Michmash'. It explained how his army used a secret path to gain access to the enemy camp. Major Gilbert went exploring and, amazingly, found the secret path. The British took Michmash by surprise, leading directly to the triumphant capture of Jerusalem on this day.

CAUGHT IN THE ACT

13 Two young men and a woman decided to burgle a department store in Frankfurt today in 1979. Then, when they passed through the furniture department, the woman and one of the men decided to celebrate their success with a frolic on a sofa. The second man asked to join in but was refused. Frustrated and annoyed, he left the store and shopped his accomplices to the police. The cops soon arrived and caught the crooks with their pants down.

BONE-HEADED BONAPARTE

14 For the 650,000 men of Napoleon's Grande Armée, the invasion of Russia in 1812 was going to be yet another triumph. Nothing could stop them. Except General Winter, as the Russians call their unforgiving weather. For six months, the French suffered from savage conditions and a lack of supplies. When the campaign ended on this day, only 27,000 fit soldiers remained. On the bright side, their defeat hastened the end of the Napoleonic Wars – peace in Europe came a little bit closer.

DEATHLY DIAGNOSIS

15 'Three months.' That's how long doctors gave 32-year-old Craig Boyden today in 1979 after diagnosing Crohn's disease. Boyden understandably decided to make the best of things, embezzling $30,000 from his employer and splashing out on fine meals, drinks for strangers and parties for his friends. This made him feel good – so good, in fact, that he got a second opinion. This doctor said he just had a hernia. After he fessed up in court, the judge decided the experience had been traumatic enough and gave Boyden a suspended sentence.

AN EARTHQUAKE INVESTIGATES

16 The New Madrid earthquakes of 1811–12 were some of the most powerful shocks ever to hit America, but, for all their destruction, they also did a nifty spot of detective work. On this day in 1811, a slave called George Lewis was murdered by his two owners. They tried to burn his corpse, but the first huge earthquake interrupted them, so they stuffed the body in a chimney. Then more earthquakes brought the chimney tumbling. The remains were exposed and the murderers arrested.

LIKE THIS, BUT BETTER

17 Matt was a cartoonist on a deadline – he needed an idea for an animated series for a TV producer. He finally came up with one in the producer's lobby.

It went down well, so Matt submitted some basic sketches, to be improved by animators during production. But the artists thought that was the intended style and simply re-traced his crude drawings. That's why Matt Groening's Simpson family had such a distinctive look when they appeared in their first half-hour episode today in 1989.

TOP CHOC CHOPPED AD HOC KNOCKS OFF SOCKS

18 If you have the odd kitchen disaster, take heart – there could be a bright side. Today in 1937, Ruth Wakefield was mixing dough for chocolate cookies in her Boston diner when she ran out of cooking chocolate. So she threw some chunks of Nestlé Semi-Sweet Chocolate into the mix instead. But what came out of the oven wasn't her usual smooth, chocolate-flavoured cookies but ordinary cookies with gravel-sized lumps of choccy embedded. Customers loved them anyway, and Wakefield had accidentally invented the chocolate chip cookie.

COMMUNICATION BREAKDOWN

19 Two robbers ran into a record store in Detroit brandishing guns today in 1994. One of them, Clive Robertson, shouted, 'Don't anybody move.' Everybody froze. It looked like villainy would win the day, until Robertson's accomplice reached for the till and Robertson, true to his word, shot him in the foot. The raid was foiled.

FAIRLY FROSTY

Today in 1684 saw the start of a frost so savage that the Thames in London froze to a depth of 11 inches and stayed that way for two months. Even parts of the North Sea froze. Bad news for ships and chilblains, but terrific fun for everyone else, who took to the ice for a 'Frost Fair'. A great street was built from the Temple to Southwark, with shops, shows and even an ox roast on a spit.

POETIC JUSTICE

Roman army commander Flavius Vespasian made a terrible mistake – he fell asleep during a poetry reading by one of history's most infamous tyrants, Emperor Nero. He was cast out from imperial favour and 'demoted' to deal with a Jewish revolt in Judea. However, Vespasian used this banishment to develop a new power base, and he was eventually declared Emperor himself today in AD 69. He then used the booty looted from Jerusalem to build one of the greatest of all Roman symbols – the Coliseum.

WE'D GIVE HIM A TICKET
BUT WE CAN'T CATCH HIM

Today in 1965, the 70 mph speed limit was introduced on British motorways. This was bad news for several British sports car manufacturers, who had routinely been using the M1 as a test track. AC Cars had driven their famous Cobra at nearly 190 mph on the motorway in preparation for Le Mans. However, for most motorists, the new speed limit was a blessing – the accident rate fell by 10 per cent.

TREEMENDOUS BATTING

23 In a cricket match in Western Australia today in 1894, a batsman hit the ball into a tree jutting over the boundary. Since the ball was in view and hadn't touched the ground, the umpire ruled 'play on'. The fielders couldn't climb the tree, couldn't find an axe to fell it, and they finally even tried to shoot the ball down. Nothing worked. A fielding fiasco, but on the bright side the batsmen ran a record 286 runs before retiring exhausted.

NOT LIKE THAT, LIKE THAT

24 It was 1947 and the young magician was making his debut. He walked on stage, the lights went up – and he immediately forgot all his lines. Every trick went wrong. It was a disaster. He bolted for the wings – where he heard the massed cheers of a standing ovation. So the magician refocused his act on comedy and within three months was on a BBC talent show. Soon Tommy Cooper was one of the biggest comics in the land.

NICE AND SPICY

25 Today in 1616, Captain Nathaniel Courthope claimed the Indonesian spice island of Run, with its valuable nutmeg forest, for Britain. Unfortunately, a spy betrayed him to the Dutch; he was murdered and his new territory seized. This irked the British and, when the nations finally signed a truce years later, they demanded recompense. The Dutch agreed to give them another small island, which they then considered worthless. This turned out to be considerably more valuable than the little spice island – it was Manhattan.

PIE IN THE SKY

26 People in the park were getting pissed off. Students were throwing empty pie tins to each other, and the whizzing discs fairly zipped through the air. If you were lucky, a word of warning was shouted – 'Frisbie!' – which came from the name stamped on the tins – the Frisbie Bakery in Connecticut. But one man, Walter F. Morrison, was more impressed than annoyed by the flying discs and he soon made a replica out of plastic. And so, today in 1967, the Frisbee was patented.

DEEPLY IMPRESSIVE

27 Three ornithologists in the Mexican jungle in 1966 were as sick as parrots – the beautiful parakeets they occasionally glimpsed kept disappearing every evening. Frustrated at being unable to find where the birds roosted, the scientists explored deeper into the jungle today – and nearly stumbled into a vast hole in the ground. They had discovered the Cave of Swallows, the largest cave shaft in the world. Its 1,220-foot deep cavern was home to thousands of birds and is now popular with climbers, parachutists and, er, parakeetists.

ARE YOU SURE THAT'S KETCHUP?

28 Earle Dickson's wife was a clumsy cook, who seemed unable to wield a knife without slashing herself. Bandages then had separate gauze and adhesive tape, and these were always falling off. Rather than have blood all over his dinner, Earle knocked up a piece of gauze stuck in the centre of a strip of tape. He showed it to his boss at Johnson & Johnson and the Band-Aid was patented today in 1926, making meals blood-free at last.

NOT TO BE TAKEN TO EXCESS

29 Today in 1676, Charles II demanded the closure of London's coffee houses, claiming they were dens of idleness. There was a massive outcry and 10 days later Charles withdrew his proclamation. The merchants who did business in these places probably decided they'd better work a bit harder, though. One of the coffee houses that subsequently flourished was owned by Edward Lloyd and was a favourite of insurance agents, and Lloyd's of London is now the hub of the modern insurance industry.

FIT ON THE FIDDLE

Norman Trangmar was very, very ill. In fact, he knew he was dying. In desperation, he used his position as an insurance clerk to swindle £28,000, which he promptly spent on his wife and children. He was caught and jailed, but Norman hardly cared – then the prison doctor realised his chronic heart condition could actually be cured. Today in 1983, Norman had an operation to fit a pacemaker and was later given a clean bill of health.

CRASHING IN

31 Evel Knievel was still a relatively unknown stunt rider when he decided to jump his motorbike 114 feet over the fountains at Caesar's Palace today in 1967. He had to use his own money to promote and film the jump. Unfortunately, he crashed on landing, crushing his pelvis, breaking his leg, wrist and both ankles, and was in a coma for 29 days. On the bright side, when he woke up he was famous, and within a year he was earning $25,000 per jump.

ACKNOWLEDGEMENTS

Thanks to my wife Rachel for her unendingly sunny support and to the Black Medicine Coffee Shop, Edinburgh, for not throwing me out even when I've drunk all my coffee.

365 Reasons To Be Proud To Be British

Magical Moments in Our Great History

Richard Happer

Come on, admit it, has there ever been a more inventive, adventurous, creative and eccentric race than the British? We don't think so and *365 Reasons To Be Proud To Be British* proves it brilliantly. In the book you'll find a historical year's worth of the discoveries, delights and derring-do that make Britain a place to love and cherish, a place of wonder and an island that attracts 27 million people through its doors. From the Cornish beaches to the glorious Welsh mountains; from the square-eyed joys of BBC telly to the incredible 'Knowledge' of the London cabbie; from our peerless pop music royalty to the globally renowned remedial powers of the perfect cuppa – Britain rules, every single day of the year.

£7.99 • Hardback • 9781907554391

365 Reasons To Be Cheerful

Magical Moments to Cheer Up Miserable Sods ...
One Day at a Time

Richard Happer

It's a well-observed fact that human beings can be a grumpy old bunch, always choosing to see that infamous metaphorical glass as constantly half empty rather than half full. Where's the fun in that? *365 Reasons To Be Cheerful* is, well, it's exactly that. It's a whole year's worth of funny and unique events that happened on each and every day – a wild, weird and wonderful journey through the year highlighting the moments that changed the world for the better as well as the delightfully quirky stories that will simply make you smile. *365 Reasons To Be Cheerful* is designed specifically to look on the cheerful side of life every day of the year – the perfect pint-sized pick-me-up in these sobering, sombre times.

£7.99 • Hardback • 9781906032968

'Too many people miss the silver lining
because they're expecting gold.'

Maurice Setter